TO *Tempt* A SEAL

A SIN CITY SEALS NOVEL

SARA JANE STONE

Entangled Publishing, LLC
2614 South Timberline Road
Suite 109
Fort Collins, CO 80525
Visit our website at www.entangledpublishing.com.

Brazen is an imprint of Entangled Publishing, LLC. For more information on our titles, visit www.brazenbooks.com.

Edited by Heather Howland and Stephen Morgan
Cover design by Heather Howland
Cover art from Shutterstock

Manufactured in the United States of America

First Edition July 2015

ENTANGLED
BRAZEN

To my husband, for your seemingly endless love and support.

Chapter One

Dresses like this lead to fantasy sex in a Vegas hotel room.

Lucia stood in front of the hotel room's full-length mirror and repeated her new mantra, determined to erase the what ifs that had followed her around for the past few weeks. What if she arrived in Vegas and the designer creation no longer fit like a second skin? What if she looked in the hotel room mirror and saw the girl she'd been six month ago? Overweight. Afraid…

She forced herself to look at her reflection in the mirror. She was still more curvy than model-thin, but the red bandage-style cocktail dress would disguise any remaining flaw. Her gaze stopped just short of her face, the one thing no amount of dieting or exercise would hide. Thank God tonight's party had a Venetian Carnival theme—masks required. Identities secret. Flaws hidden. Anyone she met tonight wouldn't have to know who she was. Who she used to be.

She placed her mask over her face and looked at herself again.

The dress offered promises of heated glances across a

crowded restaurant. And later, strong male hands determined to peel the fabric off her body. One look at this dress and the man of her fantasies would fall to his knees and give her an orgasm that she would remember for the rest of her life.

This would work. This *had* to work.

Of course, she first had to leave her hotel suite and find Mr. Fantasy. She picked up her clutch and headed for the door, armed with her wallet, a strip of condoms, and the pink Post-it note she'd written the night she'd decided to attend the restaurant opening. Her top four fantasies. If — no, *when* — she found the right man, she would check off the items on her list one by one.

Navigating the hotel's mazelike casino floor in her heels proved a challenge, but she made it to Glitterati, Vegas's newest and hottest Italian restaurant. And then she froze.

It looked as if everyone had jumped at the chance to wear a mask. Waiters moved through the crowd, offering bubbly and bite-size samples from the chef's menu. Hundreds of beautiful people milled about the space.

She reached up and touched her mask. Tonight, she belonged with them. For the first time in ten years, she could blend in with a crowd.

Her fingers found the place where the hand-painted creation from Venice stopped, revealing her skin. The dimensions needed to be just right to hide the jagged scars on her right cheek that sent men running away from her instead of wondering how she'd look in their bed. Even now, she couldn't believe what had possessed her foster father to take a knife to her face. But tonight, she would escape that dark past and the fear that no one wanted her. No one desired her.

This was her chance to step outside the box she'd built around her sheltered life. Tonight, all her months of planning, exercising, denying herself her go-to comfort foods — tonight, it would all pay off.

Tonight, someone would race toward her.

Tonight, she would live her life.

She stepped into Glitterati, accepted a glass from a waiter, and headed for the back, where the series of abstract paintings hung on the walls. She'd never met the artist, but she'd been a fan of his work since she started painting.

Vibrant colors streaked across the canvas in a layered chaos. The paintings spoke to the type of life she dreamed about living. The kind of person she wished she could be — bold and daring.

"Don't tell me you came for the artwork," a deep, masculine voice said from behind her. She closed her eyes briefly, sucking in a sharp breath at the sound that seemingly had a direct line to the parts of her body craving male attention.

Wow, that was fast. Good job, dress.

"What else would I come for?" she replied without turning to face him.

"I don't know about you, but my eye's been on a table filled with chocolate five feet away," the mystery man said.

Chocolate. She opened her eyes. Melt-in-your-mouth sugary goodness came a close second to orgasms on her list of wants.

"What kind of chocolate?" She kept her gaze fixed on the bold red brushstrokes running through the center of the first painting.

He chuckled. "I didn't look too closely. Does it matter?"

"The details are always important." Like if the man behind her filled out his suit with a body that promised to make her dreams for tonight a reality. "Milk chocolate tastes different from dark. Do they have fillings that melt in your mouth or ones that explode with flavor?"

She felt him move closer. His heat merging with hers. Without the mask, she might have caught a glimpse of him from the corner of her eye, enough to know if the man matched the panty-melting voice.

"You like things that explode in your mouth?" he said, the words a low growl in her ear.

"Yes." This man could read the phone book and leave her breathless and brimming with desire. But she wanted more than words tonight.

So she turned to face him.

And oh, God help her, she needed a taste of this man. Her lips refused to form the words "but I'm partial to caramel," because one look and she was partial to *him*.

Mr. Panty-Melting Voice had a body that begged to be explored, worshipped, and painted. From his square jaw to the way he filled out his tuxedo, he looked as if he was auditioning to be the next James Bond. Maybe he was. This was Vegas, only a hop, skip, and a jump from Hollywood. And in her humble opinion, his short brown hair and green eyes were a lethal combination.

Move over, Daniel Craig…

"I've been watching you stare at those paintings for the last few minutes," he said, his full lips offering a hint of a smile beneath his plain black mask. "Without even glancing at the chocolate fountain."

"There's a fountain?" She heard the note of longing in her voice. Chocolate, carbs—those had topped the list of diet no-no's for the past six months. But tonight, everything was on the table.

"Yes. You might have noticed if you had moved from this spot. So I have to ask, are you waiting for your date? A boyfriend?"

"No." Her breath caught on the one word. This man had to be *someone*—a movie star, a model, the perfect male specimen—he couldn't be for her.

But the thought of walking away and finding another

man to explore her fantasies? Impossible. In her mind, she would hear this stranger's voice. She'd spend the next forty-eight hours craving the deep sound, wishing she could listen to him murmur sweet nothings in her ear as they acted out her fantasies—or even better, *his* fantasies. If she walked away from him now, she would spend every minute until sunrise wondering about his top four, though she had a feeling he didn't carry around a pink Post-it note with his wicked desires spelled out.

"Good," he said, exuding honest-to-God charisma as he offered his arm. "Would you care to join me for a drink from the fountain?"

She placed her hand on his forearm and felt his muscles through the layers of his tux. Seriously, what did this man do that left him with a body to rival Hollywood's finest?

Chocolate first, then questions, she decided. If he said "serial killer," she'd at least have something to drown her sorrows. "So…"

Oh, crap, she hadn't asked his name.

"Cade," he supplied, guiding her through the maze of masked people toward the milk-chocolate fountain surrounded by a mountain of eat-me-now goodness.

"Lucia." The last trace of tension she'd sensed earlier faded when she said her name. "So Cade, did you come for the art or the chocolate?"

"Gorgeous, I came to find you."

Chapter Two

Not much distracted U.S. Navy SEAL Cade Daniels from a mission. But he could watch Lucia eat chocolate all night. And with each bite, his reasons for being there slipped farther away from his mind. The way her full lips wrapped around the strawberry left him picturing all the things she could do with her mouth. She licked the creamy coating off the berry and sighed as if the taste was a one-way ticket to the explosion she craved.

His jaw tightened, and he looked away from her lips. He'd approached the masked bombshell with a decidedly sinful fantasy in mind, but as soon as she told him her name, he'd realized he might have bitten off more than he could chew.

There was a chance he'd found the wrong Lucia. Watching her right now, a damn good one. This woman didn't come close to his best friend's description of her shy, reclusive sister from Tennessee.

The Lucia before him had curves that rivaled a fifties pinup's. He could spend a week worshipping her breasts with his mouth before moving south to explore her full hips and perfect ass. When he reached her shapely legs, he'd run his mouth up her thighs for a taste…

Fuck me. He closed his eyes as she reached for a third strawberry. *If this really is Natalie's sister, I can't touch her. I promised to obey the freaking best friend code.*

And he knew better than to go back on his word. Natalie, the feisty bartender who'd been his best friend from the moment he'd set foot in Coronado for BUD/S training, had extracted a promise when she'd called and begged him to spend his first night back in Sin City keeping an eye on her little sister. Natalie had offered a long explanation about an email from Lucia detailing her sibling's plan to pick up a stranger at a Vegas restaurant opening. Even though Natalie had had him from her first heartfelt "please," coupled with a "you owe me," he'd listened patiently, gathering information.

Plus, she was right. He had a debt to pay. He'd wanted a dog but was away from home too often to care for an animal. Natalie had agreed to semi-joint custody of Mufasa, the Great Pyrenees rescue he was pretty sure she didn't want. So he'd listened and asked for details about his target.

He could still hear the way his best friend had described her sister.

Lucia isn't your pretty, party girl type. She hates people looking at her. And she's always struggled with her weight. Picking up a guy in Vegas? That is not something Lucia would do. I'm worried she'll end up cut into little pieces and dumped in the desert.

If the masked woman was in fact Natalie's little sister and not her goddess impostor, he needed to work on his best friend's definition of beautiful.

"So, Cade," she said, her brown eyes fixed on the fountain as she dipped another strawberry. "What brings you to Vegas?"

A visit to my still bitter dad. Still bitter about what? Oh, that. Well, Mom left him ten years ago when he made it clear she'd never be as important to him as the Navy.

Didn't that say it all? Cade had held a grudge against his dad for years, but now Cade was just as dedicated to the Navy. He knew from watching his parents' marriage disintegrate that being a SEAL didn't leave room for a real relationship. He'd heard enough from his teammates on their last mission about how their wives struggled with their long deployments. Hell, Dante was probably using the downtime to file for divorce after coming home and catching his wife with the plumber.

Relationships were out. But a weekend of debauchery in Vegas with the woman in front of him? Hell, yes.

"I came to Vegas looking for a good time," he said, tracking her movements. He needed to get a grip on his *interest* and start asking the questions. He had to be damn sure he'd found the right woman.

"Good answer." Her mask covered everything but her eyes and lips. He wanted to see more, to read her expressions.

"And when you're not partying in Vegas, what do you do?" she asked. "Prepare for your role as the next James Bond?"

"No, I don't work alone."

She cocked her head as if trying to make sense of his words.

"I'm a SEAL in Uncle Sam's Navy. When I'm working, I have a team of guys who could kick James Bond's ass watching my back, covering my six at all times."

The honest answer seemed best. If she really was Natalie's sister, then the fewer lies he told her the better. But Natalie had made it clear her little sister would run if Lucia suspected he was there out of pity for his best friend's supposedly shy, overweight sibling.

She lowered the half-eaten berry. "I'm familiar with the SEALs. My sister lives near Coronado. She's a bartender at

Bottoms Up. Have you heard of it?"

"Yes, I have." And just like that, he had confirmation. This gorgeous woman was his mission, and not in a way that would satisfy the parts of his body begging to get acquainted with her curves.

"Have you ever been down to visit?" he asked.

"No." She shook her head, her long, straight black hair moving over her bare back. In another city, her red dress would have bordered on indecent. The fabric hugged her breasts, the sweetheart neckline dipping in just the right place to present a peek at her cleavage.

The front offered one helluva view. But the back blew his mind. A thick band of red fabric ran across her middle back, hiding her bra. But below that? A valley of bare skin down to the top of her perfect ass.

"This is my first trip in a while. What about you? You're a ways from home, aren't you?" she added, stepping away from him and closer to the chocolate, as if she sensed a wall rising up between them.

"From base," he said. "But I grew up in Vegas. My dad still lives here, about a fifteen-minute drive from the Strip."

The tension in her mouth faded. Cade had a feeling he would have a love/hate relationship with that mask by the end of the night. He was all for fun and games—hell, if she wasn't off-limits, he'd suggest trading it in for a blindfold—but the mask was also a barrier to reading her.

"So you're not just in Vegas looking for a good time," she said.

"I'm heading out to see my dad. But not tonight," he said. "What about you? Why are you here?"

"I came for the art. The chocolate is a bonus."

He closed the space between them and took the wooden skewer from her hand. He stabbed another strawberry and held it under the chocolate, twirling it back and forth. When it was covered, he held it up to her lips. "Art and chocolate. That's all you're looking for tonight?"

"No." She lapped at the creamy covering, swirling her tongue around the tip. It was mesmerizing. The way she savored each drop of chocolate, licking the damn thing clean before sinking her teeth into it. Strawberry juice covered her lips, and he fought the urge to steal a taste.

Screw art and chocolate. She'd come to Vegas to drive him insane.

"I came to Vegas to take risks," she said slowly, her voice low as if divulging a secret. "To try new things and find out if I'm as good with my mouth as I am with a paintbrush."

She winked at him, and his cock instantly stiffened. *Jesus.*

"I could help you with that," he heard himself saying, as though he had no control over himself any longer. Not with her. A neon warning sign that rivaled the lights on the famous Strip outside flashed in his mind. He could show her around, but learning what she could do with her mouth? He couldn't go there. But still he couldn't stop himself from saying, "I could be your guy."

Where had *that* come from? He knew better, but around her, it was like he'd lost every shred of willpower to resist temptation. To resist *her*.

She cocked an eyebrow. "Are you married?"

He chuckled. "No." As long as he was in the Navy, commitment wasn't in the cards for him. He wasn't about to follow in his father's footsteps. His father's commitment had ruined his mother. Cade wasn't about to put anyone through that.

"In a relationship?" she asked.

"I'm a SEAL, gorgeous. That hasn't left much time for anything else."

She smiled at him, her dark eyes sparkling with wanton need. "I think—"

"Lucia Lewis?"

Cade tore his gaze away from Lucia and focused on the newcomer, a tall man with salt-and-pepper hair. His suit looked expensive, but what did Cade know about clothes? Natalie had arranged for a rented tux to arrive at his hotel room this morning, and he'd agreed to wear it because he didn't have another option. His Navy whites would have been out of place in Vegas.

"Herman Schwartz," the man said. "I'm an art dealer in New York."

"Nice to meet you, Mr. Schwartz." Lucia held out her hand.

"Ms. Lewis, I assume you're here for the art."

"Mostly," she murmured.

"I was admiring the paintings when I saw you out of the corner of my eye. I have clients looking for similar pieces. Many would love to have yours."

"I'm surprised you recognized me."

"I had my assistant search the web for a picture of you. It wasn't easy to find, and the shot is mostly of the back of your head." The art dealer beamed at Lucia. "But I saw your long hair, and the way you looked at the paintings earlier—I took a chance. So tell me, do you have any pieces that would fit a glitzy New York City restaurant? There is a steak house owner who is in the market right now."

"I would be honored. If you email me pictures of the space, I can create something for your client, or send some photos of what I have in my workshop." Cade watched as Lucia set the strawberry skewer on the table and opened her small black bag. She peered inside, then withdrew a business card and handed it to her potential client.

A pink piece of paper, about the size and shape of a Post-it note, slipped out and fell to the floor beside her. Cade bent to retrieve it, his gaze lingering on her shoes. The shiny four-inch black heels were tied to her ankles with satin ribbons. He'd never had a thing for women's footwear, but he sure as hell liked the idea of binding Lucia's legs to his bedposts.

"I can do better than that, Ms. Lewis," Mr. Schwartz said. "I'll fly you out to New York."

"That's kind of you, but I don't travel much. This trip is something of an anomaly," she said.

Cade stood, Post-it in hand, and watched as the art dealer tucked her card into his wallet.

"I'll be touch with the pictures. And I hope you change your mind." With that, the art dealer walked away.

"You didn't mention that you're a famous artist," Cade said once the other man was out of earshot.

"I'm really not that well-known. Back home in Tennessee, I spend most of my time working with children. I'm more art therapist than artist." She plucked a dark chocolate square from a platter beside the fountain. "And you weren't here for the art."

"I'm taking an interest." He glanced down at the Post-it as he held it out to her. "Here…"

The words "you dropped this" vanished from his vocabulary as he read the small block letters. Top Four Fantasies for Las Vegas.

"Where did you get that?" she demanded, snatching the paper from his hand.

"It fell from your purse." He could hear the husky note in his voice. "Your to-do list for your trip, I take it?"

"I wrote that…well, I never planned to share it…it's for later." She stumbled over the incoherent explanation.

He saw the alarm in her brown eyes. "Later with whom?"

"You. Maybe. I hope," she murmured. The flirty bravado she'd displayed earlier vanished. And for the first time, he saw a hint of the woman who fit Natalie's description. Shy, vulnerable, and in need of someone to protect her.

He stared into her eyes. Panic, hope, maybe a hint of embarrassment—it was all there. The longer he looked, the more he wanted to be that man.

And break my fucking promises.

He'd been sent to watch over her, damn it. He was on a mission to keep her from finding someone to fulfill her fantasies. Making her naughty dreams come true? Not part of the job.

But he couldn't let her walk away. The thought of her searching the masked crowd for another man—

Hell, no.

That wasn't happening. Not tonight.

"What's on your list, Lucia?" he asked, knowing he needed to play the part of her mystery seducer even if he couldn't be the man to make her dreams come true.

"Number one." She drew a deep breath. "Number one is…well, it involves…"

"Tell me, gorgeous." He glanced at her purse, fighting back the urge to take the Post-it back and read the list himself. "What are your fantasies?"

"I want an irresistible man tied to my bed," she said softly. "That's number one."

The concrete reasons to keep his hands off Natalie's little sister headed for the exit. Cade heard those words— *an irresistible man tied to my bed*—and he didn't want to do the right thing. He wanted to be Mr. Irresistible and help her cross off every item on her list.

"What's number two?" he demanded.

"A man willing to…" She pressed her lips together, her fingers toying with the clasp on her purse. The bag opened with a click and she reached inside, withdrawing the pink note. "I can't say the words. Out loud." She held out the Post-it. "Here."

Cade took the small piece of paper, his fingers brushing

hers. He glanced down and read the second item.

2) A man willing to go down on me until I come so hard I forget my own name.

Desire knocked his reservations out of the building. The reasons he should stick to the plan and keep his hands off Lucia would be waiting for him in the morning. But tonight he needed to cross off the items on her Post-it.

Maybe that was his loneliness talking. Avoiding relationships, focusing on his job—it came at a cost. Sure, he had his dog and his friends, but for one weekend he'd like to take a break from the solitude his situation demanded.

After watching Lucia lick strawberries while his dick begged to join the party and reading her list, he wanted— strike that, *needed*—to spend a night or two with a woman who wanted what he had to give but wasn't asking for a future. He could find a willing partner in Sin City then go back to duty, his need slaked for now. But that wouldn't do. Not anymore. It couldn't be just any woman.

It had to be the woman in front of him. The beautiful yet shy Lucia who'd taken a chance and stepped outside her comfort zone despite the insecurities he saw rising to the surface with each passing second. If he didn't say something soon, he'd bet she'd run for the door.

She didn't realize it, but she was triggering every protective instinct he had.

"I'm willing, gorgeous," he said, his gaze moving down the list to numbers three and four.

3) An orgasm. In public.

4) Give a man a blowjob that will leave him begging for another.

He closed his eyes. After watching her eat chocolate, he had a feeling she would excel at number four.

"Cade?" she said.

He heard the uncertainty in her voice. He opened his eyes, folded the note, and slipped it into the pocket of his rented tux jacket.

I'm going to hell for this.

He took her hand and laced his fingers through hers. Then he drew her away from the fountain, his hand on her elbow, and guided them to the exit.

"Where are we going?" she asked.

"To cross number three off your list."

Chapter Three

Lucia followed Cade, the Navy SEAL she'd known for about five minutes, through the maze of card tables and slot machines. He stopped beside the trash bin bearing the hotel's logo, removed his simple black mask, and tossed it inside.

"I think I'll keep mine on," she said, her voice light and playful even though her nerves were a rioting mess.

In the restaurant, she'd felt brave and daring. But out here, under the casino's bright lights, the web of emotions that had left her sealed in Tennessee—terrified to be herself unless it was on the canvas—blocked the way.

She stopped beside a bar lined with touch-screen machines. "Maybe we should have a drink first."

Cade smiled and gently pulled on her hand. "Then we're going to the perfect place."

The sound of his voice was like a drug. Irresistible. They walked past the hotel gift shop and turned a corner. Velvet ropes lined one side of the hallway and led to a nightclub. The hypnotic beat of the music poured through the doors.

"Number three," she whispered. "In *there*?"

"Gorgeous, I'm not going to walk you into the club, make you come, and jump to the next item," he murmured in her ear, holding her at his side as they waited for the bouncer to check IDs. "I'm going to get you wet, excited, and ready first."

"Oh." She fumbled with the clasp on her purse. "How?"

He smiled, took her driver's license, and held it out to the bouncer. Then he led the way into the club's cave-like entrance. "Trust me, I know a thing or two about wild Vegas nights."

She followed him to the long bar. It was still early, but people filled the space, most clutching a drink. The women wore tight, short dresses—the Vegas uniform. But in here, she was the only one wearing a mask.

Her hand touched her covered cheek. She couldn't take it off, not if she wanted to follow her plan to the end.

"I have rules," she said.

He nodded. "I'm listening."

"Okay. Well…"

After a few seconds, he seemed to get the hint that the words weren't coming.

"There's no rush," he said. "Let's order first."

"Champagne, please," she said.

He relayed that information to the blond bartender hanging on his every word. Then, drinks in hand, they moved through the dark crowded interior to an exit.

"The outdoor space is one of the things I like about this club," he said, placing his hand on her lower back. Her skin tingled as her brain tried to form a coherent message for the rest of her body, a sane response to his touch and his voice.

Stay close. Follow him. Let him touch you.

Okay, so maybe she'd left her firm grip on logic and reason back in Tennessee.

"The club opens to the hotel's pool deck. Fresh air, music, and space to move around," he continued as he guided her toward the water. They stopped by the steps leading down to the shallow end.

"Now for your rules," he said, his body close but not touching her.

She took a long drink from her champagne. She felt his green eyes tracking her every movement.

"First rule…the mask stays on."

"I can work around it. For number three. I'm not making any promises about number four."

The familiar panic rose. "I need your word. Please."

"All right. You have it. The mask stays on." He turned to her and raised his free hand. His fingers brushed over her lips. "Are there any other kinks I should know about?"

"More kinks?" she repeated. Then she realized what he meant.

For her, the mask was a necessity, not a preference. But to him, it was a game.

She felt a wave of relief that the reason could be so simple. Easy. She didn't need to explain her desire to hide the scars that had labeled her a victim, the deep grooves that left her feeling ugly and unwanted.

As if a switch had been flipped, the bold and daring feeling she'd carried within her at the restaurant opening returned. She'd spent months planning this weekend. She'd lost weight and bought the perfect dress. And now she wanted to claim the prize. She wanted to claim him.

"Yeah," he said. "I promise to keep an open mind." And he winked at her.

"No," she said, laughing. "No other kinks." She paused. "What about you?"

"I have a few, but we'll get there." His fingers moved down her neck, and her nipples formed hard peaks, begging to be next. "Are there more rules?"

"I go home Monday, and I'm not looking to keep in

touch."

"Four fantasies in one weekend. You're asking for a lot." He abandoned her neck and wrapped his arm around her waist. "Good thing I like a challenge."

She nodded and fixed her gaze on his fingers as he traced small circles in the palm of her hand.

"I'm not saying I'm looking for more." He drew her back against the hard planes of his body, and his lips brushed her ear as he spoke. "I'm not in a position to offer promises right now. But walking away from you won't be easy. Any man in my shoes would agree."

She let out a soft moan, those words mingling with the feel of his body—she almost believed that more might be possible. But when the mask came off…

"So why just one weekend?" he said.

"Did you ever want to break free from the past and everything that made you *you*? And wish you could erase pieces of your life? Bury the memories that hurt too much?"

As soon as she said the words, she wanted to take them back. He was a SEAL, an elite soldier, the best of the best. Why would he want to walk away from everything he'd done to get there? Unless the things he'd seen and done while serving his country were too much—

"Yes." His voice was so low that she wondered if she'd imagined the word, knowing it was the one she wanted to hear. "Yes, Lucia. I have."

She leaned against him and felt every inch of his body. *Every* inch. She bit her lower lip and resisted the urge to arch her back and rub against him here, by the side of the pool in the middle of a Vegas nightclub.

"I'm taking a mini vacation," she murmured. "But I can't afford more."

"I don't want more. All I want is you, gorgeous."

When he said that word, she believed him. This man who

would look at her for all the wrong reasons if they passed on the street in her hometown, he wanted *her*. She could feel it. Maybe he craved fantasy-filled sex as much as she did. Maybe he needed her, too. At least as much as they were offering each other in this moment.

He touched her jaw and turned her head to the side, careful to avoid her mask. She stared into his green eyes and saw his unspoken question. His lips hovered close to hers. So close she could feel his breath. But she knew from the way he denied himself that final inch between their mouths he wouldn't kiss her without permission.

"Yes," she said. "Kiss me."

Like an uncaged animal, his mouth captured hers and brushed back and forth before demanding that she open to him. She parted her lips and let him in. His tongue touched hers, teasing her senses and sending her spiraling deeper into this unfamiliar dance.

She'd been kissed before. But never like this, with possession and lust vibrating through every touch of his mouth.

"Are there enough people here?" he asked, pulling back.

"Where?" She blinked, opening her eyes to the club buzzing around them.

"Out here. Dancing on the pool deck," he said, keeping a hold on her. "For number three. An orgasm. In public."

Her eyes widened. "Too many. You can't. Not here."

"Is that a challenge?" he asked mildly. "Because I could."

"No."

But he was right. She could climax right here, in this very public place, just from the sound of his voice and the feel of his body pressed against her. And oh, God, now number three felt like a mistake. The thought of an orgasm in public had seemed hot, sexy, and downright fun when she'd written the list. But now?

"No," she repeated.

He nodded, scanning the area as if looking for an escape route. He cocked his head, his gaze narrowing. "How do you feel about breaking a few rules? Not yours. The club's rules."

"Will we get caught?"

"No guarantees." He smiled down at her—and this one was wild and wicked. "But I've had some practice at covert missions."

"I've been good for a long time," she murmured, turning her head, following his gaze to the stairs leading to the upper cabana level. "I think I'm ready to be bad."

He stepped back. "Take off your shoes."

Just when she thought the low timbre of his voice couldn't get any sexier, he issued a command and brought her closer to begging for his touch. She lifted her right foot, holding out her hand for balance as she loosened the black satin bow wrapped around her ankle.

His hand caught hers, preventing her from toppling into the pool. "I look at those ribbons, and I picture your legs spread, your ankles bound to my bed."

Oh, *yes*...with every word, number three looked more and more like a reality. She pushed the shoe off her foot and let it fall to the ground. The pounding music masked the sound of the heel hitting the pool deck. She shifted her weight to her bare foot and pulled at the second ribbon.

"And then?" she asked.

He let go of her hand, lowered to one knee, and slipped her shoe off. He looked up at her as his free hand touched her calf, running up until he reached the hem of her dress. His fingers played with the fabric, drawing a gentle circle on her thigh.

"Fantasy number two," he said. "And after you come against my mouth, after I taste you, Lucia, I promise you won't remember your own name."

"Oh." The word slipped out as the picture formed in her mind. This man. Kissing her. There. *Oh, yes.*

He held her shoes for her as he stood. "Are you ready, gorgeous?"

She nodded and took his hand, allowing him to lead the way to the stairs. They reached the bouncer. The man was larger than Cade, but with half the muscle. Cade leaned close to the man's ear, careful to keep her out of earshot. The bouncer went from half asleep to alert and spoke into the radio attached to his wrist within seconds.

After the man moved away from the stairs, Lucia moved closer to Cade. "What did you say to him?"

"I may have suggested I saw someone cheating at the craps table," he said, scanning the area. Moving quickly, he unhooked the velvet rope and led her up the darkened stairs. She went willingly, excitement pounding through her veins.

"Here," he said when they reached a dark corner cabana. The doors leading to the interior poolside room appeared closed and locked, but a pair of lounge chairs covered in dark blue cushions remained on the balcony overlooking the club.

"Turn around," he murmured as he moved behind her. His fingers toyed with the straps of her red dress and lowered them down her shoulders. "And tell me what you see."

"People." She gasped as he drew her dress down to her waist, revealing her black lace bra to the night air. Her nipples pebbled, begging for his touch. "Everywhere."

Her breasts were left wanting as his hand moved to her legs and lifted her skirt until it bunched at her waist. A thrill ran through her. All those people below, and yet she was on the verge of losing herself in this moment. Being here, with him, felt wild and wanton, so far removed from the walls holding her trapped in her life back home.

"When you come…" His fingers teased the edge of her lace thong, and she spread her legs, opening for him. "When you scream my name, will they hear you?"

"No," she gasped. His finger slipped beneath the edge of her underwear. "Maybe. I don't care."

"Does this fit your fantasy? Is this what you want?" he demanded. "Tell me."

She turned to face him and looped her arms around his neck. His hand moved over her, and his fingers ran down her backside, touching, exploring. Her hips rocked against him, demanding friction.

"I want you," she said. "Make me scream your name. Over and over. I don't care if they hear. I want the fantasy. Please."

She saw a flash of hesitation in his eyes. Had she said too much? Pushed too far? But it vanished as quickly as it had appeared. Thank goodness. If he walked away now, leaving her body begging for release, she might never recover.

"I want to taste you." He cupped her jaw, and his fingers brushed the place where the mask met her skin. Then his lips claimed hers. He opened her mouth with his tongue and explored every inch. When he broke the kiss, his breath came in sharp, needy gasps.

"Jesus…" she murmured.

"How would you feel about a doubleheader?" he asked. "Two and three right here. On that chair with hundreds of people dancing below."

"Yes. *Please.*" She was begging now, but she didn't give a damn.

"Thank God." He swept her into his arms as if she was light as a feather and gently laid her down on the cushions. Some rich, possibly famous person had probably paid a fortune to sunbathe on this lounge before the hotel's pool transformed into a nightclub. And now she was lying here with her designer dress decorating her waist, her underwear exposed.

She turned her head to one side and watched as he moved to the foot of the chair and lowered down to his knees.

"Spread your legs for me," he ordered.

She obeyed, resting her head back and closing her eyes. His hands moved up her thighs and guided them apart. With one hand, he shifted her underwear to the side.

"You're glistening under the moonlight." His breath teased the parts of her body waiting and hoping for Mr. Panty Melting's kiss. "I can see all of you. And I fucking love that you're bare."

His fingers touched her smooth folds, drawing circles around her clit. Her hips bucked up, and her thighs clenched.

"Keep your legs spread," he demanded, withdrawing his hands. "Or I'll tie you up."

Heat flared in her core, and she felt the parts of her body level with his eyes pulse with need. "Do it," she whispered.

She heard movement, followed by his hands slipping her feet into her shoes. Gently, he wrapped the ribbon around her ankle and the chair's metal leg. After securing the binding with a tight knot, he moved to the other foot and repeated the process.

"Better," he said, running his hand up her bound leg.

She felt his broad shoulders, still covered by his tuxedo jacket, between her thighs. Later, once they'd crossed off a few more items on her list, she wanted to see him stripped down. She wanted to explore his too-perfect body. And maybe learn his fantasies.

His tongue lapped at her entrance. Once. Twice. And she pushed aside thoughts of his fantasies. Her world was reduced to his mouth. Tasting. Teasing…

"You like that," he said, slipping a finger inside her.

"Yes."

"Tell me," he demanded. "I want to hear you."

Her hips bucked up to meet his mouth. The sound of his

voice pushed her closer and closer. He ran his tongue back and forth over her clit, as if offering her the show-no-mercy approach to oral sex.

"Oh, God," she said. "Just like that."

"This?" His tongue traded places with his fingers. This man knew how to touch her.

"Yes," she whimpered. "Don't say another word. Please. Just kiss me."

She craved the sound of his voice, but right now, she needed his mouth on her sex. And he obliged, putting his lips on her, his tongue inside her—

The orgasm slammed into her. Her whole body arched, and her ankles pulled against her bonds. And his tongue, his fingers… Relentless.

"Cade!" she cried. "Oh, Cade, *please*."

He stayed with her, taking his cues from her body, waiting until her wild, bucking hips eased down to the chair before he drew back.

"What's your name, gorgeous?"

"Hmm?" It was all she could manage. The pleasure maintained a stronghold on her body. Music drifted up from below, mingled with voices, but she didn't care. Nothing mattered but the bliss, so much greater than she'd imagined when she'd closed her eyes and dreamed of this alone in her bed.

"I think we can cross off oral sex so good that you forget your own name. So we're two down with two to go," the rough, oh-so-sexy voice said. "And Lucia, the night's still young."

Chapter Four

Cade stared down at the woman writhing on the lounge chair and fought the urge to rip off her mask and see her glow. If he had his way, he'd carry her up to his room and strip her down so he could see every inch of her in the light before he buried himself inside her. But part of him knew he should walk away now, before he broke more of the rules he'd written for himself.

Don't get in too deep. Don't get involved. You'll only hurt her when you redeploy.

"I feel so good," she murmured. "Even after."

Except there was no fucking way he was walking away from the damn near hypnotic blend of sexy and innocent tied to the lounge chair. Not tonight.

Besides, hadn't she been clear that she didn't want anything beyond tonight?

"I want more, Cade."

His cock agreed, begging to be released. But it was too soon for number four on the Post-it note list. He wanted to draw this out, because in the morning, he would have to face the fact that he'd broken a string of promises.

The sound of footsteps on the stairs drew his attention away from the tempting woman. Out of the corner of his eye, he saw a security guard climbing the steps.

"Time to go." He knelt at her feet and untied the ribbons.

"Someone's coming?" she whispered, a note of panic eclipsing desire. "Here?"

"Security," he confirmed, drawing her up with one hand while lowering her skirt with the other. He surveyed his options and wished he could call for an extraction team so that they could fast rope out of there.

"We need to hide until the guard leaves." He took her hand and drew her away from the lounge chair and into the shadows by the cabana door. He pulled on the padlock and thanked his lucky stars when it opened. The same staff member who'd left the cushions on the chairs after the pool area closed for the night had likely forgotten to lock the damn thing.

"In here." He led her into the dark space. He angled his body in a way that shielded her and allowed him to keep an eye on the door. He could feel the rise and fall of her breasts, her chest pressed up against his.

"We're safe here," he assured her. "Even if they find us, they'll just ask us to leave."

"You've been here before?" she whispered. "Hiding from Vegas security?"

"Not at this club. But when I was younger, I had a run-in or two with the bouncers at some of the Vegas hotspots." Back when he'd run wild—desperate to get away from his parents' fighting, and after that ended, his father's pain—he'd ignored the rules, including the Nevada state laws prohibiting underage drinking. And he'd found ways to evade security *after* he'd been caught once or twice.

"But I've learned a thing or two since then," he added.

Footsteps approached the cabana, and he pressed a finger to Lucia's lush lips. Calling on his years of training, he did his best to focus on the sounds outside the door, not the woman pressed up against him. But the way her fingers clung to the lapels of his tux, as if trying to decide if she should trust him—or make a run for it—threatened to split his attention in half.

If she didn't believe he could save them from a bouncer with a flashlight, he doubted she'd relinquish her mask tonight. And he wanted to pull those strings and see every inch of her. His desire mounted the more time he spent with Natalie's little sister. He wanted—

"All clear up here," a security guard said. "The day crew left the cushions out. But I don't see anyone. I'm taking my break."

The footsteps grew distant, headed for the stairs, but Cade hung back, refusing to leave their hiding place until he knew the coast was clear.

When he felt certain they'd be spared an encounter with security, he murmured, "I think we can head down now. Follow me."

He led the way down the stairs and past the bouncers. He used his size to push through the crowds, and he kept Lucia close behind until they reached the brightly lit hallway connecting the nightclub to the hotel casino and restaurants. Ten feet away from the entrance, he turned to her and placed his hands on her shoulders.

"Are you all right?"

"I think I've had enough excitement," she said, clutching her purse. Her mouth formed a thin line, not a hint of the wanton, begging woman who'd forgotten her own name in the aftermath of her first orgasm. And he sure as hell didn't want it to be her last.

"Lucia, we're not going to get into trouble. At least not the kind that leads to answering a security guard's questions."

"I never get that close," she said, glancing back at the club.

He didn't need a peek beneath her mask to know the fear of being discovered had followed her into the casino's brightly lit hallway.

"One taste of trouble is enough," she added. "I should probably head back to my room."

"Have you seen Vegas?"

She blinked, as if surprised by the question. "I drove down the Strip on the ride from the airport. What else is there?"

"Come with me." He took her hand and led her through the casino and out into the warm Vegas night. He paused at the front entrance and glanced at her feet. "How far can you walk in those shoes?"

"Back into the hotel and up to my room." She pulled her hand away. "Which is exactly what I should do."

"Please." He signaled for a cab. "Let me show you the sights. Let's make the most of your time here. We're not going far. And you won't see anything like this in Tennessee."

She stared at him, his words sinking in.

You won't see anything like this in Tennessee.

No, she'd never see a Navy SEAL dressed in a tuxedo looking at her as if he wanted to spend the night by her side.

"Okay," she said.

He held the cab door open for her as she got inside, and then he slipped in beside her and gave the driver instructions.

"After this, we'll talk about the remaining items on your list. I wouldn't want you to go home unsatisfied." He pointed out the window. "That's Planet Hollywood—"

"Cade," she said softly. "Tonight has already been more than I ever dreamed it would be. We don't need to cross off everything."

"That's a shame, because your number four lines up perfectly with my number four."

"Your number four?" The words tumbled out on a shaky breath.

"You're not the only one with fantasies," he said as the cab pulled to an abrupt stop at the curb.

She barely suppressed a moan. What she'd give to hear his fantasies…

Do you want me on my knees? And what will leave you begging for my mouth wrapped around your cock?

"We're here," he said.

She followed him out of the cab, his supposed list momentarily forgotten as the man-made lake in front of the hotel sprang to life. Water shot from the fountains, accompanied by the familiar sound of "Luck Be a Lady." And purple light illuminated the hotel walls in the background.

"It's beautiful," she murmured as the water leaped higher and higher. "A work of art come to life."

"I thought you would like the Bellagio fountains." He moved behind her, wrapped his hands around her hips, and held her close.

"I wish I could paint this." Bold blues rushed across the center. If she could capture the awe inspired by the water's movement, the canvas would spring to life.

"Why did you become an artist?" he asked, his lips close to her ear as he held her.

"I started when I was sixteen," she said.

In the weeks after her foster father had cut her face, when they'd taken her away from Natalie and, for better or worse, away from their ugly life. Those first few days, it had felt like a downward spiral into worse. As if she'd failed. As if she hadn't been good enough. As if she deserved the mark on her face. But then the therapist had given her paints.

"Someone handed me a brush, and once I started painting,

I couldn't stop," she continued, leaving out the hows and whys linked to the scars hidden behind her mask.

"What drew you to painting?"

"I think I fell in love with bringing the beauty of a single moment or emotion to life," she said. "When I'm painting, I can break free from everything else and lose myself in what I'm creating. It's not too different from being here." She let out a low laugh. "Sin City and art—I always thought they were like apples and oranges."

"There's more to Vegas than casinos and clubs," he said. "There's beauty here, too."

Her laughter died. This place represented his home and his childhood. For him, it was more than an escape. "Did you come here, to these fountains, a lot when you were growing up?"

"They opened about fifteen years ago, when I was still in junior high school. Or at least that's the first time my parents and I came to see it. My mother loved this show."

Loved. Past tense. She glanced over her shoulder at the powerful man standing behind her. "She's gone now? Your mother?"

"No. Well, not like that." He kept his gaze focused on the water show. "She's remarried and living in Boston now. But it might as well be the moon considering how often I get out there or she comes west. I try for one holiday a year, but my leave doesn't always line up."

When she'd formed the plan back in Tennessee, intending to pick up a man, she hadn't envisioned learning about his past, his childhood, anything beyond the here and now. The man in her fantasy walked into her life a stranger and left the same way. But with Cade, she wanted to know more, to ask about his family. And just how bad had he been before?

Did she have the right to delve into his secrets when she refused to show hers?

The water show ended, and the people lined up at the railing drifted away and moved on with their nights. He remained pressed against her, his arms holding her tight.

"Ready to see what else Vegas has to offer?" he asked, his low voice teasing her senses. Every time this man opened his mouth, her body longed for his touch.

She leaned her head back against the broad wall of muscle she had yet to explore. If she had the courage to follow her plan to the end, this night might end with his tuxedo jacket on her hotel room floor, his shirt abandoned on a chair, and her fingers tracing the contours of his chest.

She stared out at the still water that had been bursting with life and movement minutes earlier, possessing a beauty she'd wished she could capture and express on a canvas. Did tonight have to be any different than a painting? A fantasy so real that she couldn't tell the difference, but when it came time to turn away, it wouldn't follow her back to reality.

"No, I've seen enough of Vegas," she said. She bit her lip, and with one hand still clutching her purse, the other moved to his thigh. "I want to see more of you."

She was stunned she'd let the words escape. Silence filled their little bubble of Vegas, the dull roar of the never-ending stream of people fading into the background as she waited for his answer.

"And then?"

"I want…"

"Tell me, Lucia," he commanded. "Tell me what you want. Spell it out for me. Every detail. Don't hold back."

His voice flamed her need and sent it roaring like a bold wildfire that refused to be contained.

"I want to add to my list," she murmured. "Number five— find a man and help him experience his wildest fantasies, the things he dreams about when he touches himself, eyes closed in the shower—"

"You'd like to see that, wouldn't you?"

She rubbed her thighs together as wet, reckless desire raced through her. "Yes. I would."

"You'd like to watch me wrap my hand around my cock and listen as I describe all of the things I'm thinking about doing to you since I first saw you admiring your paintings. You want to know what makes me hard for you." He rocked his hips into her backside, allowing her to feel every inch of him.

"Yes." She was close to begging now. "I want to work my way through your fantasies, too. Starting with your number four."

"Lucia, you found your man."

Chapter Five

Lucia slipped the hotel key card out of her clutch, but before she swiped the card, she allowed herself this final chance to ask: *Are you really ready for this?* Because once they went inside, there would be no turning back.

If she sent Cade back to his room, regret would find her as soon as the door closed, and it would follow her home. Instead of memories, what ifs would become her constant companions.

He would go if she insisted. As aggressively as he'd pursued her, he'd also respected her consent at every turn. Even about the mask. He hadn't said a word of protest about leaving it on after she'd spelled out her rules back at the club. Instinct told her to trust him, at least with her body.

And tonight, wasn't that all the trust she needed?

She swiped the card and turned the handle, and he followed her into the suite.

Beyond the mirrored closets in the foyer, the space opened up. A king-size bed stood on the left. A few steps farther was a sitting area with an L-shaped sofa and a desk facing the floor-to-ceiling windows, which offered a bird's-eye view of the Strip.

"Would you like a drink?" she asked as she led the way to the sitting area. "I could order a bottle of champagne. Or something to eat?"

"No." He caught her hand and pulled her close. His lips brushed hers. "I have everything I want right here."

She tossed her clutch on the sofa, and then she went to work stripping off his clothes, beginning with his tuxedo jacket. Every time she set a button free, he kissed her as if he wished to possess every inch of her body. The third time it happened, she gave up on undressing him and lost herself in his kiss.

But then he drew back, stepped out of her reach, and took over the task of unbuttoning his jacket and shirt. They hit the floor, followed by his shoes and pants, and he stood there in his boxer briefs.

His muscles, oh, God, his muscles…every inch of this man's body left her aching with the need to touch, taste, explore.

He raised his eyebrows and gave her a wry smile. His message was clear.

Your turn.

She reached for her zipper, but then she hesitated.

"I should dim the lights," she said.

"No." His boxer briefs joined the pile, leaving him naked in the middle of her hotel suite.

She drew her lower lip between her teeth, her body restless with desire. In the dark corners of a nightclub, her dress covering her waist, she'd been able to hide the still visible reminders that the last five pounds she'd tried to lose held tight to her hips. Her body was far from faultless. But his? Every muscle defined to perfection—

"The lights stay on," he said. "I want to see you. Naked

and on your knees." His hand wrapped around his long, hard length and stroked up and down, as though the very sight of her—clothed or unclothed—made him ravenous for her. "I need to see every inch of that gorgeous body when you take me in your mouth."

His words—the deep, rough sound of his voice—and his lingering gaze on her body made her own desire rise so high that it eclipsed her self-doubt.

Screw it.

Her hands moved to the back of her dress. Her clothes hit the floor piece by piece—dress, bra, panties—as her gaze remained fixed on his hand as he pleasured himself. His hips thrust into his touch, and she longed to take him into her own hands.

Naked apart from her mask, she knelt at his feet. His movement slowed, and she felt his gaze on her. She placed her hands on his thighs and ran them up until her fingers met his. He guided her, showed her how to touch him as her free hand explored the hard lines of his body, mapping the contours.

"I want to paint you," she murmured.

He let out a low laugh. "Not if it stops you from touching me. Right now, I'd rather give you my cock than a paintbrush."

He stopped guiding her, and his fingers moved to her hair. With his other hand, he cupped her jaw as her lips parted and her tongue touched the tip. Their eyes met, and his gaze echoed the desire pulsing through her.

"The mask is working for me right now, gorgeous." The low, raspy sound of his voice left her wanting more.

She closed her eyes and took him in her mouth, then swirled her tongue around the head, tasting him. This man who'd walked out of her fantasies and into her life, he wanted her, right here, right now, in this moment. He accepted her curves, saw beauty where she saw a body she'd hidden for so long. And he liked the mask, which allowed her to cling to that description—*gorgeous*. She loved the way he said the word, and the look in his eyes that suggested he meant it.

"Me too," she murmured, her lips resting against the soft skin she wanted to feel inside of her before the night ended. But for now, she stroked him. "Me too."

Cade stared down at the masked beauty. When he'd walked into the opening party, he'd had a plan in mind—find Natalie's little sister and keep her distracted. Instead, he'd broken his friend's trust by allowing her sister to literally blow him away with that mouth.

Right or wrong, he couldn't walk away from the chance to be Lucia's fantasy. He'd known that from the minute she'd raised the chocolate-covered berry to her lips.

But Lucia was so much more than a beautiful woman who could drive a man wild eating chocolate. He'd seen glimpses of the insecurities that haunted her. Part of him wanted to hunt down the men who'd given her reason to be ashamed of her beauty. From where he stood, every inch of her was designed to drive him freaking insane with lust. And he wanted…oh, God…

He closed his eyes and let his head fall back as she took him deep. He fought the need to thrust into her mouth as she took him in, running her lips up and down, again and again and again.

"Lucia." He opened his eyes and demanded her attention.

She looked up at him but refused to release him from between her sweet lips. Her hand stroked him, harder, faster.

"Lucia," he tried again. "I'm going to come soon. I can't hold on any longer. When I do, I want to come in your mouth, gorgeous. The next time, I'll pull back. I swear."

She let out a low sound that he felt from head to freaking

toe. It sounded a helluva lot like a yes. And she didn't let go or move away.

"And Lucia." His gaze connected with hers. "I'll beg you to suck me again. You can count on it."

She began to move, her lips gliding up and down. Her fingers followed, stroking him, pushing him closer. Her free hand ran up his thigh and around his hip. She pressed her tongue against his dick and held tight to his ass.

The pleasure took hold, demanding his attention, rushing over his body. Head thrown back, he roared. He didn't care if he woke half the hotel. His hands went to the back of her head as he thrust into her mouth.

"Un-fucking-believable," he murmured, struggling to catch his breath in the aftermath of an orgasm that made him want to slump to the ground and beg the goddess kneeling at his feet for more.

"You can cross number four off your list," he added, withdrawing his hands from her tangled hair. Caught up in his own mind-blowing pleasure, he'd made a mess of her long locks. "Only one item left. But I'm going to need a few minutes before you tie me to—"

"Oh, no," she gasped.

He opened his eyes and looked down. What was she…

Her mask.

The painted side rested against the carpet, the black ribbons loose on the floor beside her knees. She scrambled and picked the mask up. But not before he caught a glimpse of her face.

Now he understood why she'd insisted on the mask. Someone had hurt her and left the scars to prove it.

She picked up the mask and brought it to her face, but he gently put his hand on her arm.

"You don't need it," he said. "Not with me."

She slowly lowered the mask and studied his face, and he

hoped she could see his sincerity.

"Lucia," he said, shoving aside his questions of how and why she'd been hurt. That conversation would come later—assuming she wanted to talk about it at all. Right now, though, he saw a flash of shame cross her face, and he wished he knew how to convince her she had nothing to be ashamed of. Not with him. Not at all. The scars did nothing to hide how insanely beautiful she was.

But when he opened his mouth, his protective instincts came forward and one question took precedent.

"Lucia, who did this to you?"

Chapter Six

Lucia lowered the mask as her hopes and plans slipped out the door and left her alone in the brightly lit hotel room with the only man who'd ever labeled her gorgeous—a man who now knew the one secret she'd thought he'd never discover.

He wasn't the first who'd asked her this familiar question, but he was the first who didn't make her feel like he was asking out of pity.

"It's a long story," she said softly. "I can't…"

I can't have this conversation. Not with you, when I can still taste you.

She glanced down at the mask, wishing she'd superglued it to her face for the evening. Without it, she felt stripped bare, her horrid past on display. And she was still very, very naked.

"I need my clothes," she said. "And something to drink."

"Wait here," he said. "I'll get you a robe and a glass of water."

"Thank you."

She stood and listened as he moved about her bathroom. Would he press for answers when he came back?

"I should have ended this at the club," she murmured, placing the now useless mask on the desk.

He returned with two robes tossed over one arm. His other hand held a glass of water. She took one of the robes from his outstretched arm, then wrapped the soft cotton around her body. She accepted the glass of water, and as she took a drink, he put on his robe.

She almost coughed out the water in her mouth and barely repressed a laugh. On his imposing frame, the fluffy white robe looked comical. The sleeves came up short on his well-defined arms, and the robe barely closed over his broad chest. His very sexy chest that her fingers were itching to touch.

"The mask," she said, sitting down on the L-shaped sofa and drawing her legs up. "It's not part of some kinky game."

"Yeah, I figured that out." He claimed a spot on the sofa, just out of arm's reach. He leaned forward and rested his forearms on his thighs, seemingly unconcerned that the robe splayed open in the front, revealing the parts of him she'd so recently had in her hands, in her mouth.

"Look, you can tell me to mind my own business," he said. "You don't owe me an explanation. But I won't lie to you. If someone did this to you, I want to hunt that person down."

No, she didn't owe him anything. He was here for fun, wild sex. Nothing more. But looking at him now, she saw a warrior. This man was a soldier, trained to wipe out enemies. And she'd put his protective instincts on high alert.

Another man would make excuses and walk away. Most people stared at her scars, their eyes wide. If they asked anything, it was out of morbid curiosity and a big portion of pity. And then they stepped back, as if they needed to maintain a certain distance from her.

"When I find the person responsible, I'll—"

"He's in jail," she said. "It's over and done."

Except when I look in the mirror or leave the house and feel everyone staring.

In those moments, it felt as if the bad guy behind bars had won.

"Did you put him there?" Cade asked.

"Yes."

He took a deep breath. "Okay. As long as you're safe now."

She nodded, a piece of her pride returning. At least she could sit here and tell this man, this warrior, that in her darkest moment, she'd fought back. Maybe not right away. She'd been too young and weak. But afterward, when she'd been asked to press charges, to testify, she'd said yes. She'd done everything in her power to lock him up.

"Will you tell me what happened?" he asked.

Earlier, his skin to her skin, he'd issued commands with the blink of an eye. He'd demanded that she remove her shoes and spread her legs. But he wasn't giving an order now. He was asking, plain and simple. The choice was hers.

She drew a deep breath. It had been years since she'd explained her scars. The people she worked with in Tennessee knew, and the children at the hospital never asked. They were suffering from the pieces of their individual stories that had landed them in art therapy, and so they simply accepted her as she was.

Outside the hospital walls, everyone allowed her to keep to herself, spending her days painting. And most tried not to stare when she went to the grocery store. Tried and generally failed.

Cade was different. He'd looked at her with desire. He'd said the words: "I want you." But now that he'd seen the scars, what did she have to lose by telling him the whole story?

"I was in foster care," she said. "With my sister. It was our third family. The first two didn't work out. My sister—she was too much to handle. This third couple had grown children and a big ranch outside of town. They owned horses and when we arrived…I thought it was heaven. They took us in when I was sixteen. Natalie, my sister, was seventeen. Not that it matters."

"It's your story. The details matter," he said. "So you were sixteen and in foster care?"

She swallowed. Anyone else, any other time, she'd worry about the fallout of sharing this much. But wasn't that the point of this weekend? Anything she did, anything she said, it was all temporary. She could embrace a freedom she never allowed herself, and for once, she wouldn't have to worry about the consequences.

"After a few months with our new foster father, it became clear that nothing we did was good enough. Everything about having us there made him angry. I know Natalie was difficult, but that feeling that no one wants you, that you're an obligation…it hurts. I think Natalie became immune to their attempts to make her 'part of the family.' I tried. I really wanted them to like me. But nothing worked."

"He did this?" Cade demanded. "Your foster father?"

She nodded. "One day, while I was cleaning out one of the horses' hooves, our foster father came up to me. He stared screaming about what I'd done wrong, cleaning the hoof the wrong way. Usually Natalie would be there and interrupt, draw his anger away, and they'd shout at each for a while. But this time, my sister had snuck into town to meet her friends. I think he knew that, and it made him furious. He grabbed a knife that I'd left out and swung it at my face…over and over…"

His jaw tightened with each word out of her mouth. "You don't have to keep going."

Her hand went to her jagged scars. She wanted to paint the full picture for him. Beyond this room, she could count on one hand the number of people who'd listened to her story.

She needed the man who looked at her and saw beauty to understand how that label had been ripped away from her. "I'd like to finish."

He nodded. "Okay. I'm listening."

"Once my foster father realized what he'd done, I think he tried to clean up the cuts himself. I don't remember. But when Natalie came back late that night, she saw them and called nine-one-one. The doctors tried to repair the damage, but he'd cut too deep. And I was left with red, ugly scars." She stared at the carpet. "Here, in Vegas, I can hide behind a mask. But back home? Away from fancy parties and nightclubs? I can't hide."

"Lucia, look at me."

She lifted her head.

"You don't need to hide behind a mask. You're—"

"Stop. If I'd turned around in the restaurant and you'd seen my face, you would have walked away. Maybe not right away. But you would have found a polite way to leave."

"No, Lucia." He clasped his hands in his lap, interlacing his fingers. "I would have stayed."

Cade looked away, his gaze fixed on his hands. He would have stayed because he'd wanted her from the moment he'd spotted her studying a painting. Her curves, her long hair, and her vulnerability had drawn him in. Knowing why she'd felt the need to hide didn't change the fact that one look at her, standing with her back to him, had sparked his desire.

He only wished Natalie had told him the fucking truth about Lucia. Maybe then he would have been better prepared to make her feel protected and cherished the way she'd needed from the first moment.

Natalie had offered him a few details into her and her

sister's childhoods, but nothing like this. If he'd known, he would have seen the mask for what it was from the start—a defense against a world that judged her by the way she looked and found her damaged.

He glanced back at her. Even if he'd known the truth, would he have done the "right" thing? With Lucia, the lines blurred. Their wild night didn't feel wrong.

"So now you know all my secrets," she said.

And I should tell you mine. I should tell you who sent me.

But if he told her now, she'd question his every word and action. And he had a bad feeling she wouldn't believe him when he said he'd broken the rules when he'd accepted her challenge. He'd wanted to make her fantasies a reality. Hell, he still did.

Wasn't there a way to give her what she wanted and live up to his promise? Not just help her fulfill her fantasies, but make sure she explored every inch of them in complete safety.

Come Monday, they could go their separate ways. He'd talk to Natalie and tell her to keep her mouth shut. Lucia never needed to know he'd been sent here.

"You don't have to stay," she said. "You don't owe me anything." She lifted her water glass to her lips.

No, he owed her the truth, or at least the part he could give her.

"A scar doesn't change the fact that you're the only woman who can drive me wild simply by eating a chocolate-covered berry." He stood and shed his robe, then took the robe's cloth belt. He tossed the strip of fabric onto her lap, and then he turned and headed for the bed.

"Cade?"

He heard movement, the soft sound of her footsteps on carpet. He stretched out on his back, the soft comforter beneath him and his arms overhead, and smiled at her. "Time for your next fantasy. Tie me up, gorgeous. The night isn't over, and I'll be damned if I let the sun rise without crossing off every item on your Post-it."

Her fingers toyed with the belt from his discarded robe. "I don't need pity sex, or pity fantasies."

"Lucia, look at me."

Her hesitant gaze zeroed in on his face, and her hands stilled. "Okay," she said.

"I hate what happened to you. But I'm not lying here with my cock hard at the thought of you tying me up and riding me until you forget your own name out of pity."

She blinked, and he watched her focus shift lower, until she saw the proof of his desire.

"I've broken a lot of my own rules tonight," he said. "Not because I feel sorry for you. I want you. From the moment I first saw you staring at the painting, I wanted you. Come to bed, gorgeous, and claim your fantasy."

Chapter Seven

Lucia had witnessed countless people—family, doctors, strangers, the list went on—offer her the all too familiar words: "I'm so sorry." She knew pity inside and out. And Cade was right. Pity didn't look like this—a Navy SEAL with the muscles of a superhero, naked on her bed.

Her gaze drifted over the hard lines of his body. This man's body was a work of art, surpassing even her wildest fantasies. And he was still here. For *her*.

"Tell me what you're thinking, gorgeous. Did you have something different in mind for number four?" His arms moved to his sides, elbows pressing into the bed. And his upper body curled off the bed as he looked at her. "I can improvise."

"When I wrote that list…" Her gaze drifted over his sculpted abs, moving lower and lower. She'd licked every inch of his long, thick cock, reveling in the way he filled her mouth. When he'd climaxed, his hips pumping into her, demanding more, she'd lost herself in the heady rush of power.

And then she'd lost her mask.

At home in Tennessee, she'd allowed her imagination to run wild. She'd sat in her sunlit studio writing lists without thinking through the consequences.

"I'm listening," he said. "Tell me what you wanted when you wrote your list."

To run away from my past and straight into the arms of a fantasy.

Everything about this man was bigger than her dreams. "The thought of tying someone to the bed—"

"Not someone," his deep voice cut in. "Me."

Her gaze met his. "Claiming control sounded exciting. But now, with you…"

Her feet refused to carry her one step closer to the bed. Hidden behind the mask, she could allow desire and wanting to sweep her off her feet. But without it?

"The red dress," she continued. "That's not me. Not really. And I don't—"

Ride men like you until I come screaming your name.

She'd planned to keep her insecurities bottled away for the night. The simple act of spelling out her fantasies on paper had granted her confidence. She could do all of the things she dreamed about when she closed her eyes and pretended she was the beautiful, sexy woman who'd walked into Glitterati tonight.

But to do this now? They'd just dipped into reality, and he was inviting her back into a fantasy. It blurred the lines in a way she hadn't expected.

"Lucia."

She glanced up at his face, expecting frustration. He'd offered her exactly what she'd claimed to want, but instead of joining him on the bed, she'd decided to explain all of the reasons she might die from embarrassment if she actually tied up a Navy SEAL. And if she climbed on top of him, he would notice every extra pound and—

"Watch my hand." His voice drew her mental downward spiral to a halt as he reached for his cock.

He ran his hand up his thick length then paused at the top. His fingers swirled through the liquid beading at the tip and drew it down. He lifted his hips off the bed and groaned as he thrust his thick cock against his palm. But he kept his eyes fixed on her.

Oh, he was good. He'd seen how watching him touch himself excited her. Now she ached to replace his hand with her own. To abandon her robe and climb on top of him—before he changed his mind about the woman who'd invited him into her hotel room and then left him to take care of his own needs.

"Cade, I can't—"

"Just watch," he said, and his deep baritone seemed to send a vibration all the way through her. "I don't give a damn about the dress. I'd tear it to pieces to get at what's underneath. Without you, that dress does nothing for me. But on you? The way it revealed just enough to leave me dying to slip my hands underneath and feel your perfect ass…"

The intensity in his eyes bordered on overwhelming. His free hand moved between his splayed legs and cupped his balls, drawing them down.

"Open your robe." His words hovered on the line between a command and a plea. "Let me see you."

She dropped the tie from his robe to the floor, and then she drew her robe back, exposing her breasts and widening the V-shaped opening to her waist. The belt remained snug around her stomach, hiding the parts of her body that left her second-guessing why a man like him would want her.

"You're fucking gorgeous."

She let his eyes linger on her, soaking up his desire. What was he thinking about her while he looked at her? While he touched himself? "What about you? What are your fantasies?"

He sat up. "I look at your breasts and I want to bury my cock between them. Let's call that fantasy number one."

The blatant appreciation in his green eyes spoke to the part of her body silently pleading with her to join him on the bed. "And number two?" she murmured.

"Reach down, below the belt, and open your robe."

She drew in a deep breath and pulled back the fabric. Her thighs had never been fantasy material. But the groan coming from the Navy SEAL on the bed told a different story.

The sound reignited the bold feelings she'd carried into the restaurant with her. She drew the robe wide open.

And his hand froze midstroke.

"Cade?" she whispered.

"If I keep going, I'm going to explode." Deep, dark desire shined in his eyes, the kind that turned a tuxedo-clad superhero into an animal. "When I look at you, the things I want to do—hell, I'll need more than one Post-it note."

"Tell me," she demanded.

"Fantasy number two," he said. He wasn't touching himself anymore, but his cock rose back to attention anyway, irrefutable proof this man wanted her. "I'm dying to slide inside. I'd settle for straight-up missionary. But since this is my Post-it list, I'd lay you down, your breasts pressing into the bed. I'd take you with my hands on the ass I've been admiring all night."

His words were like a drug, and the intoxicating sound of his voice doused her doubts in a haze of longing.

"Number three," he said with a playful smile. "I'd like to revisit the scene at the nightclub."

"The people below," she said. "They turned you on?"

"You did. Tasting you drove me wild. I don't give a damn about the setting. I'll make you come with my mouth buried between your legs any damn place you choose. Give me a day and I'll prove it. I'll go down on you in bed, at a club, by the pool, in a closet—any location that turns you on and leaves you wet, I'm game."

His gaze shifted up her body to her face. Instinct demanded she turn her damaged cheek away.

"Lucia, look at me." His words were filled with a deep wanting. Not a hint of a threat. And she turned back to him. "I meant what I said by the fountain. My number-four fantasy lines up with yours. I look at your mouth and I fantasize about your lips."

When she looked in the mirror, the woman who stared back at her, haunted by the past—she wasn't fantasy material. But maybe if she narrowed her focus to her mouth and her breasts, if she concentrated on the pieces of herself that turned him on, she could slip into the illusion for a few more hours.

Cade patted the bed. "Come here, gorgeous, and let me kiss you."

As she bent over the bed, her breasts spilled out of the robe's wide opening.

Look at me, touch me, lick me.

The words spun on the tip of her tongue. She glanced up at him and reached for the discarded belt from his robe.

"Do it," he said. The gleam in his eyes bordered on feral. "Pick up the tie and bind my wrists before I come just from looking at you."

She took a tentative step forward. "Lie down flat."

His abs contracted as he leaned back and stretched his arms overhead.

She paused at the foot of the bed. "Close your eyes," she said softly.

For a second, she thought he would protest. But he simply took one last look, his gaze lingering on her breasts until anticipation rippled through her. And then he obeyed and rested his head on the comforter.

With the robe still covering her waist, she climbed onto

the bed and crawled to his wrists.

Do I dare?

In the morning, the fantasy might shatter into a million pieces. But he was here now. And he wanted her.

Her gaze dropped to his thick cock. Thinking of how he'd touched himself, she wrapped her fingers around him.

"Last chance to tie me up," he growled, his hips lifting into her touch. "Do it now."

She released him and slid the bathrobe tie under his wrists. The headboard didn't really offer a place to wrap the cloth around. Unless she wanted to bind him to the nightstand, she would have to settle for tying his wrists together. She completed the bow and knelt beside him, admiring her work.

"With your training, you could probably break free anytime you choose," she said, her gaze moving over the six-foot-plus Navy SEAL on her bed.

"In a heartbeat," he confirmed, opening his eyes. "But those training exercises are about escaping a situation. Right now, the last thing I'm looking for is a way out."

His words were measured and controlled. But the wild look in his eyes begged for unrestrained satisfaction.

She bent over and kissed him hard. She pressed her palm against his chest and ran her hand over his abs. Her hair fell forward, covering his face and chest. As she deepened the kiss, her fingers brushed the tip of his cock, and she moaned against his lips. She wanted him just like *this*—the need clear and present in his green eyes and her body on fire with yes-I-dare desire.

He broke the kiss, and his chest rose and fell as he drew in quick, measured breathes. "No more teasing."

She sat up, the hint of a smile on her face. "No more."

She slipped off the bed and retrieved a condom from her purse. She rejoined him, straddled his thighs, and tore the foil packet open.

"Don't play with me," he warned. "I haven't been this close to losing control since I was a teenager."

"I can't wait any longer," she said, feeling the truth of her words through every inch of her body.

She rolled the condom on him, savoring his fierce groan. With one last glance at the wicked, wild fantasy lying bound beneath her, she positioned him beneath her and sank down.

His hips thrust up, punctuating his sentences. "I need you to hold on tight. This is going to be hard and fast. Next time, I'll take it slow. I swear. But right now, I'm out of my mind."

"Don't hold back," she murmured, leaning her head back. She matched his frantic pace, grinding her body into his. The robe flowed around her like a cape. And right now, in this moment, she felt like the perfect match for the superhero SEAL bucking beneath her.

She fell forward and placed her hands on his chest. Her world narrowed down to the feel of him filling her...the pressure against her clit...the pleasure. There was no space here for her past and her insecurities. Not with this man taking her.

"Oh, God," she whispered.

"Say my name again," he barked, pumping into her.

She felt him straining toward the end goal, no longer bothering to hold back. Maybe he'd climbed onto her bed with a road map, an idea of the right way to do this. But she had a feeling he'd abandoned it, losing himself to base need. Losing himself with her...

The thought brought her to the edge, too, suddenly, powerfully. She screamed his name as she collapsed on his chest, her legs trembling from an orgasm that deserved a place in the record books. She closed her eyes, determined to memorize this feeling, the sensations bound to this place, and to—God help her—this man.

"Cade," she whispered. "Cade."

"Right here with you." He thrust up one last time. A low groan filled the room, his body tensing and straining beneath her. And then he stilled, the only movement the rise and fall of his chest as he gasped for air.

Slowly, she sat up, their bodies still joined as she stared down into his warm eyes. The desire had faded, replaced with something that looked an awful lot like awe.

"Hi," she murmured.

"We've moved a helluva long way past hello." His voice set off an aftershock pulsing up through her. "You just rode me to the best damn orgasm of my life."

"The best?" She wrapped the robe around her body and sat beside him on the bed. "You don't have to say that." He was sweet to compliment her, but one red dress and a list of fantasies did not make her Bond girl material.

"You might not believe me now," he said, sitting up and easily slipping his hands free from the bow that looked as if it belonged on a present, not a SEAL. "But it would be my pleasure to prove it to you tomorrow."

He stood and headed for the trash, his back to her as he disposed of the condom. He turned to face her with his hands on his hips and his head cocked. "Assuming you want me to stay."

She'd expected him to pull on his pants and head for the door. The thought of sleeping in his arms and waking up to his voice, his body, and oh, heaven help her, his words…

If she said yes, she might start to believe the fantasy. And when she stepped onto the plane Monday afternoon, it would hurt that much more. But she'd learned to live with pain and rejection before. It was the pure pleasure that was new to her. She wouldn't let this opportunity slip her by. Who knew when she'd have a chance to live out a fantasy like this again?

"Yes," she said. "Stay with me."

Chapter Eight

Walking into a Vegas breakfast buffet dressed in the tux he'd worn to last night's opening—minus the bow tie—screamed walk of shame. And shit, today he had a damn good reason to hang his head in disgrace. He should crawl into the doghouse for breaking his promise to his best friend. And for hiding the truth from Lucia.

He'd done a lot of things that rode the line between right and wrong while serving his country, but holding back from Lucia felt like a new low. Yeah, he was pissed at Natalie for hiding pieces of her sister's story. But his anger was like a fine sheet of ice. Beneath the frozen surface, his heart broke for what his friend had suffered.

Natalie was tough now, but he hated the fact that she'd been forced to develop her don't-fuck-with-me attitude as she'd been passed from one foster home to another. And after hearing her story, he suspected Natalie shouldered a share of the guilt for their foster father's actions. Hell, maybe Natalie had been protecting herself as much as Lucia by keeping these things secret.

His phone vibrated against his leg, and he withdrew it from his tuxedo pants. *Please don't let it be Natalie.* He needed to talk to Lucia's sister, but not before breakfast.

He glanced at the screen, spotted his home number, and moved away from the crowd gathered by the plates. "It's my dad. I need to take this, but it won't take long."

Lucia nodded. "I'll wait for you."

He held the phone to his ear. "Hey, Dad."

"Cade!" His father's voice boomed through his phone. "When do you get into town? My calendar said last night, but I know how these things change. I can't wait to see you, son. I made a list of things we can do to make the most of your leave."

"I'm here. I arrived last night, but I had plans."

"Oh." The excitement vanished from his old man's voice.

Cade winced. He could picture his father counting down the days until Cade's leave. Hell, as a kid, Cade had done the same thing. "But I'd love to meet up later and fill you in. In fact, I could use your help."

"I don't know how much advice I have to offer these days," his father said. "Does this have something to do with your team?"

"No. But I know you can help. Pick a time this afternoon that works for you and shoot me a text." Cade glanced at Lucia waiting patiently to the side of the buffet line. "Right now, I've got to go."

He ended the call, slipped his phone back in his pocket, and headed for Lucia. "Ready to eat?"

She smiled. "Starving."

They moved to the end of the buffet line. A tall, slim woman in a pink tank with the word "Angel" written across her chest turned to Lucia and offered a plate from the stack. The angel let out a soft gasp but quickly covered it with a fake smile.

"Thank you," Lucia murmured. She turned her face and kept the scarred side out of the woman's view.

He picked up a plate still warm from the dishwasher and fought the urge to snap the china in two. The casual glances thrown in their direction as he'd walked through the hotel in last night's tux took on new meaning. He placed a hand in the small of her back and guided her forward. The woman in the pink shirt bypassed the hot food and headed straight for the fruit.

Lucia's gaze followed the other woman. Her eyes narrowed for a moment, but then she looked away. Shit, she'd lived with that for years. No wonder she didn't bother letting it show how much the woman's expression must have hurt. Witnessing it firsthand, he wished he could shield her from that kind of pain.

"I'm having potatoes," she said, her voice low as if divulging a dirty secret as she spooned home fries onto her plate.

"And biscuits," he said, his mouth close to her ear. "Don't forget those. Or the bacon."

She glanced longingly at the biscuits. "Those are made with real butter. And they're packed with flaky, melt-in-your-mouth carbs."

"How about I take two and you can have one off my plate? That way the calories don't count," he said, recalling a fling with a woman who'd had a strong aversion to carbs. But only when they touched her plate. Everyone else's food was fair game. Of course he'd tried that trick with Natalie once and she'd told him that if he ate off her plate she'd slap his hand away.

"No." She reached for the biscuits. "I want my own."

He followed her through the rest of the buffet, watching as she turned her face away from curious glances and smiled at the few people who made eye contact. The look in her eyes was reminiscent of an apology. He swore her reaction to the stares was more instinctual than intentional.

It happened again as they wound their way through the tables, but this time for a different reason. A man in an "I'm in Love With Love" T-shirt looked at Lucia, and she smiled. Except lover boy wasn't focused on her face. The man's gaze lingered on her chest.

Cade shook his head. No wonder she had trouble trusting his desire for her, not when she was accustomed to people treating her like an object, not a person. No concern for who she was. What she wanted. How she felt.

He moved to her side and blocked the guy's view. He wrapped an arm around her waist and guided her to a two-top against the wall. His actions screamed *mine, mine, mine* to anyone glancing their way.

"What's on your Post-it note list for today?" he asked once they were seated.

She looked at him over the top of her biscuit. "I've been dreaming about a lounge chair by the pool, my book, and a strawberry daiquiri with an umbrella in it."

He could picture her in a bikini that barely contained her breasts and her mouth wrapped around a straw. "Do you like fruity cocktails more or less than chocolate?"

"More." She took a bite and closed her eyes. "I've stayed away from daiquiris, piña coladas, chocolatinis, and oh, God, biscuits for the past six months. I've been trying to be good—"

"Not today." He reached for his ice water. "Vegas isn't the place for good. Trust me."

"And what happens in Vegas stays in Vegas, right?"

"Not the memories." Six months from now, he had a feeling that when he closed his eyes, he'd see her mouth. The memory of her lips wrapped around a berry—or hell, his dick—would follow him halfway around the world.

And he hoped she'd recall every touch, every kiss and

remember how it felt to be cherished, her body worshipped for hours. In his eyes, a few cuts didn't rob her of the beauty she'd been born with.

But it had stolen her confidence. Watching her walk through a room filled with strangers without her mask, he had a feeling there were moments when she wanted to disappear.

"I'm not going to forget last night," she said, her voice firm.

"Or today. I'm going to make your dream come true at one of the best pools in Vegas," he said, the pieces of a plan quickly falling into place.

She raised an eyebrow. "What makes it the best?"

"There's a beach with real sand," he said. "I have a friend who handles the cabana reservations. He should be able to hook us up without having to slip past security."

"What about your father? Isn't he expecting you?"

"We talked about getting together later, but he'll understand if I need to rework the schedule." He focused on layering his biscuit with eggs and bacon. "My dad was in the Navy. A SEAL. And believe me, he always made the most out of his downtime. He loves Vegas and everything this city has to offer."

Ball games, camping trips, and even the occasional concert at one of the Vegas hotels—his dad treated leave like one big celebration. His mother had enjoyed their adventures in the moment, but Cade knew it had made it that much worse when he left again. Everyday life dulled in comparison. And the fear that his dad might not make it back had loomed over them month after month.

"So you're following in your father's footsteps?"

Hell, I hope not.

When Cade looked to the future, he saw battles fought overseas, not shouting matches at the kitchen table about why serving in the teams trumped damn near everything else.

"Your dad must have really loved his job," she added. "For you to want to join the Navy, too."

"He did," Cade admitted. "He carried the honor on his sleeve. After my parents split, I had to see what it was about. So I joined."

"Did you figure it out?" she asked.

"No," he said, biting into his biscuit.

Enlisting in the Navy had changed his life. But he'd never been able to pinpoint why his father had risked his marriage to serve. After his first year, he'd stopped looking for reasons. He'd chalked his mother's request for a divorce up to the fact that the realities of military life took a larger toll on the family members back home than most people realized.

"Then why stay?" she said.

"I learned why I love serving my country." He set his self-made breakfast sandwich on his plate and focused on Lucia. "It took a while. At first I just wanted to be the best. But even before I joined the SEAL teams, I knew what I was doing was important. Maybe not my day to day, especially in basic training. But I was surrounded by guys my age who were ready and willing to risk their lives to protect people."

"When you put it like that, everything's dwarfed in comparison," she said softy. "You'd inspire anyone to join up."

He laughed. "Especially when you're seventeen and fresh out of high school. Before I left Vegas, my idea of freedom revolved around taking my parents' car for a night, or sneaking out of the house to fool around with a girl. But now I've been to places where most of the freedoms I took for granted as a kid, they don't exist."

"It changed you," she said.

He nodded. "I woke up to the fact that I wasn't in the Navy for myself or for my dad. I fought to join the SEAL teams because serving is the right thing to do. Even if at the end of the day, it just means some punk gets to fool around with a girl in the backseat of a car. At least they get a chance to be kids."

"Wow," she said.

"Yeah." He glanced at her. "I bet you're regretting asking that question."

"No." She looked him straight in the eyes. This time she didn't turn the injured side of her face to the shadows or dip her cheek to her shoulder. "I go to work at the hospital every day because helping kids who have seen the worst of what life has to offer, giving them a chance to find their way back the same way someone helped me—it's the right thing to do. I can't erase their pasts. But I can give them a paintbrush. I can offer a creative outlet that tells them their voice matters."

"I'm so damn glad someone gave that to you." He stared across the table and focused on her as he pushed the images of war out of his head.

He'd seen shit that made his skin crawl. Kids carrying guns. Young girls wearing suicide bombs. But he couldn't let those memories stop him from living his life or doing his job. The best way to fight it was to focus on the present—and the woman he could protect from all the hurtful glances.

Sometimes when he was in the line of duty, it was hard to remind himself that while he couldn't change the world, he could make a small difference in the lives he touched. That's what he would do for Lucia. Maybe he couldn't transform her life, but he would offer her the kind of life she deserved for this weekend. He would make sure she felt cherished. Desired. Valued.

"It sounds like there's a lot of you in your art," he added.

"Some of the pieces." She picked up the last bit of biscuit. "I've done a few paintings for restaurants or corporate offices. Painting as a form of therapy is rewarding. But so is earning a paycheck. Without the added income, I couldn't afford designer shoes."

"Your shoes were pretty damn close to a work of art in my book," Cade said, dropping his voice low. "But I would love to see your paintings someday. Not the ones you make for others. The ones you paint for yourself."

"Maybe." The corner of her mouth offered a hint of a smile. "But first I need another biscuit."

"Done." He pushed back from the table and paused beside her chair. He locked away the haunting images his job had left behind. Today, he needed to focus on Lucia. Maybe this weekend, they could be each other's escape. "And I'll get you something sweet while I'm there just to watch you moan with pleasure."

Lucia stole a glance at Cade's perfect butt and allowed the delirium of the moment to sink in. She'd just sent her very own Navy SEAL to fetch her a biscuit. She mentally ticked off the list of times this man could have walked away from her—after the club, when her mask had fallen off, before they fell asleep in each other's arms—but he'd stayed.

Her cell phone buzzed, drawing her attention away from his perfect backside. She found her phone in her purse, nestled beside her crumpled Post-it. She scanned the text message on the screen.

Need to know you're okay.

She smiled. How many text messages had she received over the years from her sister that began with those words? It drove her sister crazy that she couldn't take down Lucia's demons. But her sister always checked in. And if Lucia needed her, she knew her sister would find a way to help.

How was last night? The opening? Tell me you didn't

go through with the plan.

She glanced at Cade as he surveyed a table littered with breakfast pastries. She'd had that perfect male specimen tied up beneath her last night. Looking at him now, her plan seemed like the best idea she'd ever had. With a laugh, Lucia turned back to her phone and started typing.

I'm so much better than okay, Nat. Don't worry. I went ahead with it and met someone.

Her reply came back within seconds. One word.

DETAILS.

She chuckled and texted back:

He's a SEAL! Six feet tall, a wall of muscle, and a voice designed to melt a girl's panties.

"How do you feel about doughnuts?" Cade's deep, sensuous voice teased her senses as he approached the table.

"We were friendly until I accused a Boston cream of forcing me to need Spanx. So now we try to steer clear of each other," she said as he set a plate piled with doughnuts of all shapes and sizes on their table. Chocolate glazed. Vanilla and sprinkles. Powdered sugar. "I should probably keep it that way if I want to wear the dress I brought for tonight."

"I won't try to convince you." He pulled the plate closer. "Now tell me more about this dress."

She laughed, a giddy feeling rising up in her chest. He said those words as if he had every intention of sticking around to see her wear it. "It's the most unusual shade of blue. I've never seen such a vibrant color."

"Blue. Got it," he said. "And the neckline?"

"Low," she admitted. "But it's the back that might lead

to trouble."

His gaze sharpened. "What kind of trouble are we talking about?"

The familiar sound of a phone beeping to indicate a new text interrupted. And they both reached for their cells.

"I asked my dad to suggest a time to get together," he explained, scanning the screen and setting his cell on the table. "I should hear back from him soon."

"It was my sister." She set her phone aside to read the message later. "I texted her earlier, letting her know I was alive and okay."

His hand froze over the plate of doughnuts. "Did you tell her about me?"

She nodded. "It's not every day you meet a man who makes your fantasies come true."

"She knows about your Post-it list?" He sat back in his chair and picked up a chocolate glazed doughnut.

"Not the list, but—"

The beep sounded again. She leaned forward and scanned the two screens side by side. It was for Cade. And she didn't try to read it. But one word caught her eye.

DICK.

All caps.

"Um, I don't think this is from your father." She held out the phone before she was tempted to scan the screen and find out who'd sent the message.

He took the phone, his brow furrowed, and read the one-word message. "It's from a friend, reminding me that I should have called."

She smiled, leaning forward, offering a glimpse down her shirt as she reached for her coffee. "Take your time. The doughnuts and I will be waiting."

His gaze dropped to her cleavage before returning to her

face. "I'll be back. You can count on it. And then I'm taking you to the beach."

He stood, his cell pressed to his ear as he headed for the exit. After he disappeared into the hotel hallway, she picked up her cell and read her sister's text.

Did the SEAL talk you out of your panties?!

The memories from last night swirled in her mind. But she'd known from the moment he'd looked at her and called her gorgeous in that deep baritone that she would hand over her underwear. And the longer he stayed, the more she wanted to believe he meant what he said.

Yes, she typed. *And I plan to hand them over again tonight.*

Chapter Nine

Cade paced up and down the brightly colored carpet, the phone pressed to his ear. The wild pattern was giving him a headache—or hell, maybe it was the fact that in a few rings, he would get the shit verbally kicked out of him by his best friend.

He glanced through the latticework separating the buffet from the rest of the casino. Head cocked to one side, Lucia contemplated the last doughnut before picking it up and sinking her teeth into it. She quickly returned it to the plate as her tongue ran over her lips, wiping them clean.

Fuck me, I want her again. Right here, in the middle of the damn restaurant, pressed up against the wall—

"Damn you, Cade!" his best friend yelled into the phone.

"Nat—"

"How could you? I sent you to watch my shy little sister in a place where she's completely out of her element...and you sleep with her?"

"I'll give you shy, but your sister can hold her own just about anywhere," he said. "And she's a knockout. She doesn't see it, possibly because her own sister looks at her and sees an overweight woman with scars on her face that she feels the need to hide behind a damn mask."

"Did you sleep with her before or after you found out what happened?"

He could hear her stacking glasses in the background, and he had a feeling she was close to hurling one against the wall.

"I'm not giving you the details," he said. "But I'll tell you this. When I found out, I couldn't walk away from her. I couldn't let her believe even for a second that the scars on her face made a difference in how I saw her."

"How do you think she's going to feel when she learns that I sent you to the party to watch over her?" she snapped.

"She's not going to find out." He stopped in the middle of the carpet and squared his shoulders. "She's leaving tomorrow. Until then, I plan to show her around town. After she's gone, she never needs to know I'm your friend."

"What if she comes to visit me here? Everyone here knows you're the closest thing I have to family around here. Hell, we have a dog together."

"I didn't get the sense you were that close to Lucia. You've never once gone to see her in Tennessee. And she's never flown out to see you."

"We text and email," she said.

"But you've never mentioned my name."

"We've grown apart over the years. After some of the stuff that happened, it was just easier to live our lives. But I'm still the person she calls. When it matters, I'm there for her," she said, her voice trembling.

He had witnessed his petite friend stand up to drunken sailors twice her size. Nothing shook her—except the past. It was part of the reason they'd become friends. They both knew what it was like to hold grudges for the way the past shaped the future. And they both knew what it was like to have someone walk away from you repeatedly.

He leaned his shoulder against the wall. "Why didn't you tell me how bad it was for you when you were a kid?"

"I didn't have it nearly as bad as Lucia," she said softly. "No one ever laid a hand on me."

"You could have told me," he said.

"I didn't want you to walk up to Lucia at a party and offer her pity. She's had enough of that. She'd just walk away. She was looking for someone to make her feel pretty. I thought you could charm her without losing your clothes, seeing as you *promised* and all."

"Things got out of hand." *There was this list…* "And I'm sorry," he added. "For going back on my word."

"Don't do it again, and maybe Mufasa and I will forgive you." The Great Pyrenees barked in the background.

"Hey, don't bring our dog into this," he said, wondering for the hundredth time why he'd let her name their dog after a *Lion King* character.

"Fine. But from this point forward, the clothes stay on. I don't want you to get her hopes up. Because I swear, if you leave her wanting more, if you break her heart—"

"I won't. She was clear from the beginning. One wild Vegas weekend. This ends when she gets on the plane."

"The part where you talk her out of her panties ends now," she insisted. "The clothes stay on until she heads home."

He stole another glance at Lucia as she licked the last of the powdered sugar off her lips. Men were staring, but it didn't have a damn thing to do with her scars. He'd bet they were wondering what she would feel like under their touch, how she would respond to a kiss.

He knew. And he wanted to learn so much more.

"Cade?"

"I need to go," he said. "I've left her at the table too long. Take care of Mufasa, and I'll see you when I get back."

"You'll talk to me before then," his friend said. "And

remember, the clothes stay on."

"'Bye, Natalie."

He hung up without answering her request. He refused to make a promise he wasn't sure he could keep. Hell, he'd try. But one glance at Lucia and he knew there was no way he'd be able to get through today without feeling her skin against his at least one more time.

• • •

Lucia surveyed the beach built in the middle of the desert. Lounge chairs lined the sand. About half were filled, but it was still early by Vegas standards. And in the distance stood a three-story building with floor-to-ceiling windows. Through the glass, she spotted bikini-clad dealers standing behind gambling tables.

The sun shined high above the desert beach. Thirty minutes on a lounge chair in the July heat and she would be ready for a visit to the air-conditioned casino. Or maybe a swim. Assuming she found the courage to strip off her knee-length black dress and abandon the wide-brimmed hat currently shading her face on the chair.

The hat didn't hide her face, but it would hopefully help her avoid some of the blatant stares. Still, men and women glanced up as they walked past, some looking longer than others.

"One-piece or two?" he murmured, leaning close to her. He'd traded his tux for navy-blue board shorts that hung low around his waist and a gray T-shirt with the words "The Only Easy Day Was Yesterday" on the back.

"What?" Her body responded to the deep growl of his voice. Beneath her suit and cover-up, her nipples yearned for his touch.

"Your bathing suit," he said. "I can't stop thinking about what's beneath your dress."

"One-piece." She looked out at the water. Three women wearing small pieces of fabric masquerading as bathing suits splashed in the waves. Blonde, with slim waists and full breasts threatening to escape their suits with each movement, they looked like a scene out of Barbie's day at the beach.

Cade tossed a towel over a chair and spread another on a second chair for her. "Want a drink? First round is on me."

One of the Barbie girls was now looking in their direction. The first one had caught her friends' attention and was now pointing at them.

"Ignore them," he said.

But she studied the woman's face, her pouty lips parting as if she might start drooling. "They're not looking at me."

"Good," he said, spreading his towel over the chair.

"No." She settled onto the lounge chair. "I bet they're debating who should come over first. Or maybe they're planning to ambush the sexy sailor on the shore."

He glanced over the bikini trio and then behind them, as if seeking another target. "I don't have 'SEAL' tattooed on my forehead."

"It's your muscles. They're like a homing device. I bet this happens all the time."

"Yeah, I walk into war zones and the bad guys are drawn to me and my biceps," he said, offering a taste of dry wit that combined so perfectly with his deep voice.

"Joke all you want, but they're heading this way."

The trio walked out of the ocean as if auditioning for a swimsuit commercial.

I bet they bypassed the biscuits on the breakfast buffet.

He spared them a glance before returning his attention to her. The laser-like focus in his green eyes formed a lethal combination with his devilish smile. As soon as he opened his mouth, she would melt into a puddle of simmering, burning need.

"I have a plan to distract and redirect the enemy," he said.

She raised an eyebrow. "If the Navy sends you out to defend our freedoms against girls in bikinis, I'm beginning to see why guys are willing to suffer through BUD/S training."

"Guys join because they want to be the best," he said. "So, are you in?"

Out of the corner of her eye, she saw the trio moving closer. "I'm in."

"Take off your dress and lie down on your stomach," he ordered.

She hesitated. The suit showed so much of her. Maybe not as much as the ambushing Barbies, but she had more to hide.

"Don't second-guess yourself, gorgeous." The timbre of his voice dropped so low, she felt the rumble from head to toe.

In one swift motion, she pulled off the cover-up, revealing her plain black suit, and rolled over. She laid her hat and her dress by the chair and turned her damaged cheek to the towel.

"Are they distracted yet?" she murmured.

"Not yet. We're just getting started."

He stood and slipped out of her view. A second later, she felt his leg brush the outside of her thigh, and his knee pressed into the chair. He swung his other leg over until his body hovered over the tops of her thighs. He leaned forward and rested his hands on either side of her torso, palms pressing into the towel, close enough to brush the sides of her breasts.

"Did you bring sunscreen?" he asked.

"I put it on before we left." Her low back arched into him, and his hard length pressed against her. He flexed his hips, and the pressure offered a taste of the hard, deep thrusts from last night. Only this time, they were still dressed on a public beach.

I've never hated bathing suits this much. All that fabric…

"We'll have to pretend," he murmured, sitting up and stealing away the delicious pressure.

She moaned in protest and lifted her head, straining to look back at her hard-bodied torturer. "Is this part of the redirect?"

"No. This is the part where I show every person on this damn beach that the only pleasure I care about is yours." He placed his hands on her shoulders and rubbed small circles over her bare skin. "Pretend I have suntan lotion."

He lowered his hips and rocked against her once, twice… then he rose up.

"This is the redirect." He swept his hands down her back, his fingers dipping beneath the sides of her swimsuit, brushing her breasts. Her back arched, hovering over the chair, asking for more because this was Vegas, the capital of wild and wanton. He granted her silent request by cupping her breasts.

"Oh…" she whispered.

"No one in her right mind would think I'd be interested in anyone but you," he said as he returned his hands to her back.

His words were the sweet cherry on top of the decadent and downright naughty thrust of his hips against her backside.

"The women in the water," she gasped. "Their lips were shot full of some kind of plumper. I'm not sure they're in their right minds."

He ran his palms over her shoulders and planted them beside her face. His body hovered over hers, and his lips touched her ear. "Are you saying I need to work harder?"

"Yes." She closed her eyes, blocking out everything but him. "Oh, God, yes."

"We can't take this too far," he murmured. "Out here."

"You started it."

His hips ground into her. Ten more seconds and she would be on her hands and knees demanding that he take her right now.

Nine, eight, seven, six, five, four, three, two—

"We need to stop." His firm voice dashed her hopes of

reaching one. He shifted off her midthrust and reclaimed his chair. "But if you look out there, you'll see our plan worked."

Oh, no, he didn't get to leave her one second away from begging for sex on a lounge chair, feeling *satisfied* with the fact he'd driven the women away.

She lifted her head and stole a peek at the beach. He was right. The women had vanished. And she desperately wanted them back. Maybe once they realized the hard-bodied Navy SEAL had reclaimed his own chair they'd try again. He would be forced to return to the plan, taking it one step farther. His mouth on her neck, his hand disappearing beneath her suit, teasing her...

"You want them to come back, don't you?" he said with a low laugh.

"Yes," she admitted.

Because I want more of you, hovering over me, touching me.

He laced his fingers behind his head, putting his biceps on display. Those muscles were like catnip. She glanced out at the beach and spotted a heavyset man probably pushing seventy wading into the water. Where were the Barbie doll look-alikes when you needed them?

"Some things are off-limits," he said, his tone taking a turn toward serious as his gaze focused on the water.

"Like sex on the beach?" She sat up, scooping her sunhat off the ground and placing it on her head.

"Yes." He swung his legs over the edge of the chair. "I'll go get us some drinks."

She angled the brim to cover her face and stared at the man who'd taken her senses by storm. He'd turned her world upside down by offering acceptance coupled with a sexual desire so potent that his name was linked to one word in her mind—orgasm.

"Don't worry, gorgeous," he called as he headed for the bar. "I haven't forgotten about the umbrella."

Chapter Ten

Cade stood close to the bar, cursing the fact that his board shorts didn't hide a damn thing. But it was nearly impossible to hide the aftereffects of his plan. And his mind refused to forget the feel of Lucia's ass pressed against his dick. Thanks to their little show, the need to have all of her, taking her every way she'd allow, rose up like the waves crashing onto the mock beach.

But this wasn't about him. Glancing over his shoulder, he searched the sea of chairs lining the beach. The space was filling up quickly now that it was approaching noon. He spotted Lucia stretched, wearing the dress that looked like it belonged at a funeral. Every muscle in his body primed for action, ready to march over to her chair and banish her self-doubt to the ends of the freaking earth. When he looked at her, he saw the woman who had arched into his touch, not giving a damn if anyone saw. And he wanted her to feel that way again.

He turned back to the bar, unable to shake the sensation of being trapped in a hot zone without an extraction plan.

He'd already betrayed his best friend's trust once. He should honor Natalie's request and keep his clothes on and his hands to himself.

But Natalie wasn't here. If she had been, maybe she would understand why he couldn't keep his hands off Lucia. It wasn't just about his own lust, though she'd inspired plenty of that. He wanted Lucia to feel gorgeous inside and out, free to be herself without hiding behind a mask.

Shit. I sound like the freaking Mother Teresa of insecure women.

If the guys heard him trying to justify his altruistic reasons for taking Natalie's little sister to bed again, they'd send him to the team shrink, convinced he'd lost it after their last mission.

And yeah, sliding his dick against her perfect ass had nothing to do with helping her find her inner beauty. He fucking wanted her. She'd offered one more night. And he planned to take it. He'd deal with the fallout later. Minimize the damage come Monday.

There was always the chance Natalie wouldn't find out. And if he ran a little recon in advance, he'd be better prepared for the consequences.

"Here you go," the bartender said. "One frozen strawberry daiquiri and one beer." He set the drinks on the counter. "Anything else?"

"Yes." He smiled at the twenty-something woman behind the bar. "I need an umbrella for the daiquiri, a pad of Post-it notes, and a pen."

"Of course," the bartender said with a smile that assured him she'd heard far stranger requests. "I'll be right back."

Minutes later, he returned to their chairs and held out a daiquiri outfitted with two little umbrellas. Lucia sat up and reached for the glass, but he lifted it higher. "First, lose the dress. I want to see you. You're too beautiful to hide behind that black bag."

"It's not a bag." Her gaze shifted between him and the drink. "It's just not one of those skintight designer creations."

"Please," he said. "Let me see you."

He waited until the dress hit the sand before handing over her drink. She leaned back against the propped-up chair, wrapped her lips around the straw, and sucked.

Her mouth is a work of art.

Before he gave in to temptation and replaced the straw with his lips, he pulled out the pad of Post-its he'd stuck in his pocket.

"Post-its?" She held the straw close to her lips.

"I'm writing my list." He set the paper on his thigh and got to work illustrating his hopes and dreams for today, tonight, and every hour until she headed for the airport.

"You told me your fantasies last night," she said, eyes widening.

He tore off the top Post-it and placed it on the towel-lined chair. "Gorgeous, I have a lot more than four."

"Oh." Out of the corner of his eye, he saw her lips capture the straw and suck. He focused on the paper. The sound of the waves splashing against the shore filled the quiet.

"You said you had a sister in Coronado," he said, looking up from the paper. "Ever thought about coming to visit? We have drinks with umbrellas down there, too."

"We do better living our own lives." She swirled the straw through her drink. "After the incident, I buried myself in art. I think she struggled with how to help me. Natalie likes to be the one in control, the one who finds the solution and makes it happen. And she couldn't do that for me."

He nodded. Her description fit the tough-as-nails woman who served a room full of sailors and soldiers night after night, always determined to call the shots.

"We did a girls' weekend in San Francisco last year. And we talked about getting together for the holidays. But Natalie couldn't get away from work."

"Maybe next year?" he asked, removing the second Post-it and placing it beneath the first.

"Maybe. Right now we keep in touch over text and email. And she's my go-to person to contact in case of an emergency. But I'm not sure we're ready for another trip together. She has her ideas about how to move on with life, and I have mine." She took a long drink from her daiquiri. "Why the sudden interest in my sister? Is that one of your wildest fantasies? Two sisters?"

"No." His grip tightened on the pen. The thought of Lucia and…oh, hell no. He stifled a chuckle and ripped off the third Post-it.

"That's a long list for one night," she said.

He looked up from the fourth note. "What time is your flight?"

"Three in the afternoon."

"We have this afternoon, tonight, and the morning. You're mine until you set foot on that plane. Agreed?"

"Yes." She bit down on the straw.

He scribbled as fast as he could. Notes four, five, and six joined the train of yellow sticky notes.

"But I might not survive tonight," she added.

He laughed as he put the finishing touches on the last item on his list. After making sure the pieces of paper were attached, he offered her the long line of fantasies.

"I'm going for a swim," he said, pulling off his shirt. "Take your time reading through the Post-its. We'll start with your favorite."

She nodded, her eyes roaming over his chest. He tossed his shirt onto the chair.

"And Lucia," he said.

"Yes," she murmured, her gaze glued to the place where his board shorts met bare skin.

"Be honest."

He turned and headed for the water. Most days he'd rather take a dip in the ocean than a Vegas wave pool. The Pacific was bigger and better. But here, she would be waiting for him when he got out.

He waded out to the deep end and dove under, swimming fast and furious. He focused on the strokes, trying not to think about the fact that right now having her nearly trumped everything else.

Lucia looked down at the Post-its and burst into laughter. Stick figures stared up at her from the yellow paper trail. He'd illustrated every one of his fantasies.

Still giggling, she studied number one. The female stick figure—as least she assumed that was long hair sticking out from her circular head—was on her back, and the male figure had his cock nestled between her breasts.

In the second one, the stick drawing with long hair knelt on all fours with the male behind her.

Stick figures do doggie style.

And he'd printed the words "with you" in block letters next to the drawing. She glanced down the Post-it trail and realized he'd repeated those words beside each stick figure couple, confirming that every fantasy on his list revolved around her.

She lowered the graphic Post-it trail to the chair then drained the rest of her drink. She'd written out her fantasies picturing a blank face, running through wicked daydreams one after the other. The idea of people nearby had excited her. The thought of a man bound to her bed, all hers for one bliss-filled night—she'd wanted that.

And he'd granted her every wish last night. Her fantasies

now had a face and a voice. But when he'd offered his list, she hadn't expected humor running hand in hand with her deepest desire: a man who was in this *for her*.

If she was reading his stick figures correctly, he wished to take her in every possible position. Missionary, doggie style, tied up, hands loose to explore, licking her, thrusting into her mouth, and sixty-nine. Plus, he'd granted her the right to choose her favorite.

She glanced over the top of the Post-its and spotted him diving into the waves. He was at home in the water. And her home was in the landlocked state of Tennessee, a long, long way from the California coast.

She scanned the list again. The decision came with a heady sense of power. Where did she wish to start? And what did she want to save for last?

The question pulled at her as she felt the weight of that word—*last*. This time tomorrow, she would be packing her bags and heading for the airport. Her sexy SEAL and his buffet of sexual fantasies would be a memory.

Cade dove deep, then surfaced a few seconds later and drifted on his back. He floated with the current, and his perfect abs glistened in the sunlight.

Thoughts about tomorrow and the day after that faded into the background. Right now, she had the chance to make his stick-figure fantasies come true. She set aside her empty drink and stood. She covered the slips of paper with her hat and walked to the water.

She waded out into the sunbaked waves and headed for her SEAL.

"Picked your favorite?" he asked.

"Number three, please," she said in the same voice she used to order from the drive-through menu.

"If we do that here, I'll drown."

"I thought going down under the water was a SEAL

specialty." She paddled hard to keep her head above the man-made current.

"I must have missed that lesson in BUD/S training," he said, easily floating beside her.

How did he make it look so effortless? Her legs were burning, and she was barely keeping her head above water. Swimming beside him felt about as sexy as a ride on the elliptical machine.

He swam up behind her. "How about I take you to shore and we find someplace a little more private?" He wrapped his arm across her chest and drew her back against his hard body. "Not a lot. Just a little taste of privacy."

"Your plan sounds better," she said, allowing him to pull her to shore. She could have swum the short distance, proving to herself and anyone else who was looking that the past six months of workouts had left her in decent physical shape. But then she'd lose the feel of his chest against her back and his breath against her neck.

He shifted his body, relaxed his hold, and moved his hand across her chest. He trailed a light, teasing circle around one breast and then the other. Through her suit, her body begged for more.

"You can stand up here," he murmured.

Her feet touched the bottom as he ran his hand over her shoulder and down her arm, entwining his fingers with hers.

He led her out of the water and stopped beside their chairs. "You'll want your dress."

"And the list?" she asked, pulling the black cotton cover-up over her head.

"I don't need a diagram for number three." His low words left her wet and ready. "I know where I'm going."

She grabbed her bag and took his hand. "Show me."

He led her into the hotel lobby. They wound through the slot machines and past the reception desk. He moved like a man who knew where he was going, and no one questioned them as they headed for the elevator banks.

"I need your room key card," he whispered, drawing her close to his side.

"It won't work here." But she pulled it from her bag and handed it over.

Smiling, he wrapped his hand around the key. He flashed only the top of the plastic to the hotel security guard. And he kept walking without waiting for the uniformed man's approval. At the elevator bank, he drew her close and captured her lips.

She sank into the kiss. Her surroundings slipped away until she heard the ding of the elevator doors. Then he broke their kiss, led her into the elevator, and handed her back the key.

"Same color key cards, just different hotel names printed on them," he explained, hitting the button for the forty-second floor, one level below the top.

Her anticipation rose with the elevator. His hand moved to her low back. They passed the tenth floor, and the impact of what she was doing hit her. She'd known him less than twenty-four hours, yet she was following a man who slipped past security on a whim up to God knew where.

Go. Trust the man who let you bind his wrists and ride him until you were out of your mind with pleasure.

"Why not the top floor?" she asked, her interest in his answer fading as his hand moved lower.

"I don't have the key to access the penthouse level." He gave her backside one last squeeze as the elevator doors opened. "This way."

He took her hand and guided her down the hall. His gaze darted from left to right, as if surveying the options. Apart from the breathtaking view of the Strip when they stepped off the elevator, the corridor looked like any other hotel.

Doors lined either side of the corridor. Room service trays piled with the remains of breakfast sat outside one or two. It was completely ordinary, yet her anticipation spiked with each step.

He stopped in the middle of the hall and drew to a halt beside her.

Oh, God, he's going to make me come in the doorway of room 903.

"In here," he said, leading her past a sign that read ICE.

The small, white-walled room held an imposing stainless steel ice machine that jutted out into the space. When they reached the far side of the humming ice maker, he pressed her against the wall until the doorless entryway disappeared from her line of sight. Her world narrowed to the fluorescent lights above, the sound of ice falling into the holding bin, and her need to follow his fantasy to the end.

He dropped to his knees. His broad shoulders blocked the view of her lower half if anyone came by looking for ice and discovered them. Her breath caught at the thought, and her thighs pressed together as she glanced toward the hall.

"There's a chance someone might walk by," he said, running his hands up her calves. "But I promise they'll hear you before they see you."

His hands glided under her dress. Muscles that until last night had only worked during a torturous Pilates class tightened, and her core begged for attention. She leaned against the wall and felt the vibrations from the ice machine to her right.

It was a gentle hum that bore a stronger resemblance to a car moving over the road than a washing machine's spin cycle. The trembling wall teased her senses but would never deliver satisfaction. But Cade's hands—roaming her inner thighs, moving higher and higher beneath her cover-up— those hands might drive her straight into orgasm territory on their own.

She reached for the hem of her dress, ready to strip it off under the room's bright light. One step closer to delivering a fantasy that felt more hers than his.

"No," he said, his hands moving higher, reaching the top of her inner thighs. One finger slipped beneath her bathing suit and brushed the bare, damp skin beneath. "The clothes must stay on. Press your hands against the wall."

She released her cover-up. What did he mean by "must"? Was it because someone could walk in? He'd written "with you" on the note, as if he wanted her. All of her. Just as she was. As if he wanted to see *her*.

His finger teased her slick folds. "Spread your legs. Let me in."

She heel-toed her right foot closer to the stainless steel box. His finger rewarded her and slipped inside.

"Cade," she moaned.

"Hold on tight, gorgeous. We're just getting started."

Chapter Eleven

The ice machine rumbled to life, and the sound of falling cubes echoed in the small room. Cade felt the vibrations pulse through Lucia, and her body tightened around his finger. He glanced up and watched her close her eyes and rest her head against the wall.

"Oh, wow," she murmured.

He raised an eyebrow. He'd never gone head-to-head with an ice machine for a woman's attention. But he'd be damned if he'd finish second to a vibrating wall.

He hunched his shoulders, slipped beneath her dress, and prepared for battle. His lips touched the soft, smooth skin of her inner thigh as his free hand pulled her swimsuit aside. He brushed her clit with his finger, and she thrust her hips toward him, away from the wall. Now that he had her attention, he replaced his finger with his mouth and ran his tongue over her.

Stay with me, gorgeous.

Last night, he'd learned what drove her wild. He was ready and willing to give her what she wanted—and maybe a little more. He left his mouth focused on her clit and let his hand wander around her hip and slip beneath her suit. He palmed her backside and traced the path his dick had taken earlier on the lounge chair. Only this time, there were no barriers.

Her lower back arched into his touch. His fingers moved closer and closer to his target. Lucia moaned, her hips bucking back and forth, demanding more from his mouth and his hand. The low, throaty sound coming from her mouth sent blood rushing to his crotch.

He wanted to take her right here, to hell with the list and his promises to keep the clothes on. When he'd asked for Post-its at the bar, he'd wanted to erase any doubts in her mind that she drove him off a cliff named desire.

But now, with her clit grinding against his tongue, her movements urgent and needy, he'd make damn sure she walked out of this room fucking glowing. He'd give her an orgasm that would follow her around like her new best friend, daring anyone to look at her and see anything but a sensual knockout.

And he planned to stay right by her side, taking on strangers who glanced at her and thought the scars, or the full curve of her body, made her somehow less.

"Cade!"

Her palm hit the wall over and over as her hips bucked against his face, leaving no doubt about how much pressure she wanted. And he gave it to her, licking, sucking, pulling her closer.

The sound of her hand against the Sheetrock overtook the ice machine. But nothing compared to her cries for more filling the small room. He'd witnessed a woman coming hard. Hell, he'd felt this woman explode against his mouth. But this was off the charts. Right here in the hotel ice room, she wanted everything he had to give. She wasn't holding back.

"Oh, yes," she panted. "Cade. *Cade.*"

He fucking loved the fact that she connected her pleasure with his name. And then the warning bells rang. He could give her this, but nothing more. That hard truth cut into his triumph. He'd never wanted more than a moment. But with her, it didn't feel like enough.

Don't be selfish.

What did it matter if this might not be enough for him? This wasn't about what he wanted. What he needed. This was about her.

Her body tensed, and her hips stilled. She let out a low moan, hitting the wall one more time. With his head hidden beneath her dress, he couldn't see her face. But he could damn well imagine her lips parting, her eyes closing as the pleasure hit her, wave and wave.

Slowly, her orgasm eased off and her hips stopped begging for more from his mouth and his fingers. He released her ass and slipped his hand out of her suit. He rocked back on his heels and dipped his head out from underneath the hem of her dress. He stood and watched as she slid to the floor, her back pressed against the now quiet wall.

Her long black hair fell over her flushed face. Her breasts rose and fell as she struggled to catch her breath. But her eyes remained open and focused on him. Her surprise mingled with a naughty satisfaction. And her mouth—those lips formed a teasing, tantalizing smile.

Beside them, the machine fell silent. After the heat from their last round, the ice maker had probably produced enough to keep the floor stocked for the rest of the day and into the night. But one look at Lucia and he knew he couldn't wait that long to deliver her here, to this blissed-out place again.

"Between you and the ice machine..." she murmured, "that was the best orgasm of my life."

Just wait. I can do better. And I'll do it without the help of a machine.

"For the record," he said, "this one doesn't count."

"I can still feel it. It counts." She stared up at him as she smoothed her skirt over her bent legs.

He took her hand and drew her up. His gaze locked with hers, noting the lingering pleasure in her eyes. "I like that look on you. But next time, I want to be the only one to put it there. I don't like to share."

He might not have a claim to her beyond Vegas. But until she stepped onto the plane, she was his.

Her brow furrowed. "You're jealous of the ice maker?"

He laughed. He loved seeing her smile at his joke. "Maybe. But I'm glad you liked it." He reached out and brushed a strand of long black hair out of her face. "I'm asking for another chance to make number three come true."

"Now?" Her eyes widened.

"No. Now, we gamble," he said, lacing his fingers with hers. He'd already wagered his friendship. Why not risk something he could afford to lose? A hundred bucks at the craps table wouldn't hurt too much. "I promised you the full tour of Sin City."

She rose up on her tiptoes and touched her lips to his. Part of him wanted to push her back up against the wall and head straight for fantasy number five. But then she drew back, leaving him with the memory of a soft, simple kiss.

"This is the best vacation ever," she said, smiling up at him. "Thank you."

Her words mixed with the light in her brown eyes and the glow on her cheeks. And the combination sent his emotions scrambling for cover. It was too damn tempting to wrap her in his arms and offer more. But he couldn't go there. In his world, relationships were like quicksand. Even if they could keep their heads above the surface, what would happen when she found out he'd been sent here to find her?

She'd never trust him again. With her body, her heart, or

anything else. This ended in the morning. Sin City was the only place he could push his luck. Beyond the famous Strip, he had to play by the rules.

"Let's go," he said, leading her out of the ice room. "Before we attempt number two on the ice room floor."

Lucia glided through the beachfront casino as if she'd been granted wings and a one-way ticket to heavenly bliss courtesy of Cade and an ice machine. No rose petals and champagne followed by gentle caresses for her. She was the woman who'd let a big, buff Navy SEAL go down on her while exploring parts of her body she'd never dreamed about sharing, especially not in a public place.

A giggle escaped her as they walked past a blackjack table. The blonde, bikini-clad dealer glanced up and smiled, as though she recognized the look of a woman still feeling the aftershocks of an orgasm that rivaled an earthquake. Groundbreaking. Earth-shattering. Something so powerful and intimate that even the scars on her face couldn't keep two people from appreciating.

Lucia's giggle turned to laughter.

"Planning to let me in on the joke?" Cade asked, looping his arm around her waist and holding her close.

"That orgasm," she said. "It was intoxicating. I feel giddy, maybe even tipsy."

He looked down at her. "Sure it wasn't the daiquiri?"

"I'm sure." She struggled to keep a straight face. "I'm officially drunk on sex."

"Perfect time to teach you to play craps." He led her toward a large oval table with high edges. The fabric stretched over the center was covered with numbers.

Three men in bathing suits lined the table's curve. Sure,

they weren't wearing much, but the logos on their swimsuits suggested they lived in a very different income bracket. And all three had tall stacks of chips in front of them.

She slowed her steps a few paces from the table. "I can't afford to play for high stakes. Art therapy pays well, but not enough to secure a place with the high rollers."

"The table has a five-dollar minimum bet on one side and a hundred on the other," he explained. "I suggest we start with five, seeing as you're tipsy. And I'll cover your buy-in. Some chips to get you started."

She stopped a few feet from the table. "I can't take your money."

He leaned over and pulled his wallet out of his pocket. "One condition—I get to help you spend your winnings."

"And if I lose?" she murmured, stepping up to the table.

"I've had the pleasure of watching you play." He set a stack of twenties on the table. "Consider it part of the full Vegas tour."

She took the chips and set them in the groove on the table's lip as she studied the foreign numbers and markings on the felt. A plastic disk rested on the number five. And there were various sections labeled thing like "come" and "pass line."

"Five is point right now," he explained. "I'd recommend betting five dollars on the pass line for this next roll. Get a feel for the game."

After a nod from the dealer, she set the chips on the letter *P* and two more on the *C*.

"Couldn't resist?" he said.

"When given the choice, I always like to bet on coming."

He laughed. "Today, you can count on it."

His deep voice momentarily stole her attention from the roll of the dice. But then the small group at the table cheered and drew her focus to the table as the dealer added more chips to her pile.

The game moved quickly after that. Hovering at her side as if he were her personal bodyguard, Cade offered a few words of explanation and the occasional suggestion.

"What should I do for the come-out?" she asked him after a player on the far side of the table rolled a seven.

"Your choice. I think you're getting a feel for the game now. And I need to step away and make a call," he said. "I'll swing by the bar for another round of drinks. What would you like?"

"For gambling with the next James Bond? A kir royale," she teased.

The bikini-clad woman taking bets did a double take and looked at Cade long and hard, as if trying to determine if she had a movie star at her table.

He noticed her glance and caught Lucia's eyes. "Not my style, gorgeous. You know that," he said, pressing a kiss to the nape of her neck. He whispered into her ear, "And you put every Bond girl I've ever seen to shame."

Her Navy SEAL moved away from the table, and she felt some of the afterglow follow him. She turned her focus to the table and watched the dice flying through the air.

Cade wanted her. Out of all the beautiful women in Vegas, he'd handed his stick figure fantasy list to her. He'd taken her to the ice room on the forty-second floor and given her an orgasm that deserved a place in the record books. He'd thrust past her inhibitions and introduced her to a level of pleasure she'd never imagined.

As she placed her bets, she stole a glance around the table. Three men on the far side of the table were staring at her. The dealer who'd studied Cade moments earlier smiled.

She's looking at me like she knows what we did in the ice room.

Cade returned to her side with a champagne flute. His

voice was low as he moved behind her and grazed her ear with his lips. "I promise you everyone at this table is wondering what I did to put that wild look in your eyes. Did I bend you over the bed before we left the room? Steal you away to a quiet corner and press you up against a wall until you screamed my name?"

"They'd be getting warm with option B," she murmured, then leaned forward to place her bets. She'd added another thirty dollars to the table, but when she withdrew her hand, she couldn't recall where she'd set her chips. The feel of Cade at her back shredded her focus.

"But they don't know that I can still taste you," he said.

"Cade—"

"Those guys over there just got one helluva view when you leaned forward," he continued. His hand went to her waist and glided up her torso. "Lean back."

She rested her head against his shoulder, offering him a peek beneath her cover-up. "I like to look, too," he said. His fingers teased the neckline of her cover-up. "But I want more. I want to take you back to your room, ask you to close your eyes and pretend all of these people are watching while I pour champagne over your tits and lick them clean."

She tried to focus on the game. If she didn't, she might be tempted to strip off her clothes and beg him to take her here.

"After I get you wet..." he continued, "I want to cross number one off my list. I want to slide between your breasts until I come." He drew a path to the center of her chest.

"Yes," she said, struggling to maintain a calm expression.

"Awfully stoic for someone who just won," the dealer said.

"Won?" She looked at the table as the dealer added the piles of chips she'd bet. "Oh my God, Cade, I didn't lose your money. I more than doubled it."

She did a celebratory dance, shifting her hips from side

to side as she leaned forward to gather her winnings. Behind her, Cade groaned, and his hands glided down her sides until he had a firm hold on her hips.

"Gather your chips," he ordered, and the heels of his hands pressed against her ass. "It's time to move on to the next stop on your tour."

"And this time the clothes come off?" she asked, standing up, her hands filled with chips.

"Yes." His gaze lingered on her chest. "But not in the way you're thinking."

Chapter Twelve

The cab inched down the Vegas Strip toward their hotel. Out the window to her right, the Eiffel Tower—miniature version though it was—glimmered under the afternoon sun.

"Are you going to give me a hint about what's waiting for us back at the hotel?" Lucia asked.

He sat with his arms crossed, his hands hidden behind his military-issued biceps. While she appreciated the view, he hadn't touched her since they'd left the casino. After he'd spelled out his down and dirty desires by the craps table, he'd kept his hands to himself.

"The anticipation is killing me," she added.

Of where he'll touch me next... How his hands will move over my skin... What he'll ask of me...

"Do you like surprises?" he asked.

"Sometimes," she said. "But not when they pile up like this."

He cocked his head and furrowed his brow. "Pile up?"

"I don't know where we're going." She angled her body to face him and placed her hand on his thigh. "For all I know, you might ask for number one right here in the cab."

His jaw tightened as his gaze dropped to her chest. "I can't. It would ruin my plan for the rest of the day."

"Which is?" she prompted, running her hand up his thigh. "You told the driver to take us back to the hotel. Is it number four in the shower? Or do you want a repeat of number three?"

"If I touch you now, it'll be number two in the back of a cab," he growled, the muscles in his thigh contracting beneath her touch. "Hell, I'm tempted to rent a limo with a divider and tinted windows just to get you on your hands and knees while we drive around Vegas."

"We could use my winnings." She brushed her hand against the part of his body she was dying to free from his board shorts.

"I have plans for your money."

"Tell me," she insisted.

"I want pleasure to dictate your life until you step foot on that plane tomorrow, not fear of what others think," he said. "You deserve to feel worshipped. From head to toe." He caught her hand and lifted her fingers to his lips. As he brushed a soft kiss over her knuckles, the cab pulled up in front of their hotel.

"Worshipped?" It felt like a big word for a Vegas fling. And one she couldn't connect to the hundreds of dollars she'd won at the craps table today.

"I'm taking you to the spa." He lowered their joined hands. "I called in a favor from one of my mom's friends. Her name's Anna. She was able to secure a massage appointment for you, followed by a visit to the salon she oversees here."

"Cade," she said as she followed him out of the cab, "I didn't win that much."

"Anna threw in the salon visit on the house." He took her hand and led her through the resort's buzzing lobby toward the elevators.

Once inside the hotel, he turned to her. "I can cancel if you don't want the massage, or if you hate the idea of a stranger messing with your hair."

"I've only been to a spa once. But I have nothing against massages or fancy salons," she said, still reeling from this surprise gesture. He'd offered sex at every turn, but this act took fantasy to a different level.

"Good." He led the way out of the elevator and down a hallway lined with golden Buddhas and jewel-toned drapes. Every detail screamed *the Zen starts here!* as they approached the reception area.

He smiled at the young woman behind the desk. She was armed with a computer and a grin so charming Lucia couldn't tell if it was fake.

"Checking in for one massage and a hair appointment," he said.

"Name?"

"Booked under the name Cade Daniels. Anna from the salon made the arrangements."

The receptionist confirmed the details in the computer, then asked for Lucia's shoe size. She disappeared behind a curtain, then returned moments later holding a robe and a pair of slippers.

"Right this way, ma'am." The receptionist opened the door leading to the massage rooms and held out the robe. A second girl was waiting inside. The receptionist said, "If you'll follow her, she'll show you where your masseuse will pick you up for your treatment."

"Thank you." Lucia rose up to her tiptoes and brushed a quick kiss across Cade's lips. Then she turned to follow the receptionist into the ladies' waiting area. When she reached the door, she glanced back at him. "I'll see you after?"

Part of her wondered if he'd vanish while she was inside. A

movie-star look-alike who wanted to pamper her seemingly tipped the scale from fantasy to delusion.

"Of course. I'm meeting up with my dad. He's watching the game at one of the bars nearby. But I'll be back before you're done here. And I'm taking you to dinner once Anna finishes with you," he said, his voice so firm that it nearly erased her doubts. "I'll meet you at the room. This isn't over, gorgeous. I promise."

She shook her head. "It just feels too good to be true. I can't believe that out of all the people in Vegas, I found you."

His eyes narrowed, and his smile faltered. For a split second, dread washed over her. It was too close to a dream. Too good to be true. She was missing a piece of the puzzle...

"It's not a dream," he said, as though he could read her mind. "You should have all this and more. Now go enjoy the spa."

Cade watched the door close behind her.

I'm a liar.

He should tell her the truth. She hadn't found him. He'd been sent to keep her out of trouble. But he knew what would happen. She'd mentally page through the past twenty-four hours, questioning every word and every touch. And he refused to let his reasons for searching her out strip away why he'd chosen to stay.

His cell rang and drew a pointed stare from the woman behind the desk. Understanding the warning—don't mess with the serene spa experience—he headed down the Buddha-lined hall, the phone pressed to his ear.

"Jack, what's up?" he greeted his teammate.

"You need to get back here," Jack said in his easygoing Southern drawl.

"I miss you, too, sweetheart," Cade said, allowing sarcasm to infiltrate his words. "But I'm a little busy here."

"Cute," Jack said. "But I'm not calling because I miss your face, sunshine. Dante's drunk and disorderly. He's talking about pictures of some plumber's junk on his wife's phone to anyone who will listen. Your girl Natalie has already threatened to kick his ass out of the bar if he doesn't get his shit together."

"Ah, hell." Cade paced back and forth in front of the elevator bank. After their last mission, Dante had returned home and learned his wife was having an affair with the man his teammate had hired to fix the kitchen sink. And the news had sent Dante into a downward spiral.

Jack could talk Dante off a cliff. Shit, Jack had literally helped his teammate scramble down a jagged mountain in Afghanistan three years ago. But with Natalie involved? His teammate and his best friend were like oil and water on a good day. The fact that Cade had slept with Natalie's little sister wouldn't tip the scales in Jack's favor today.

"Ask Natalie to cut him off," he said.

Jack snorted. "She did. An hour ago."

"Then get him out of there," he ordered. "Do whatever you have to do. But get him away from the bar. And then just listen to whatever he needs to say. His marriage is over and he's trying to deal with the heartbreak."

"What the hell do I know about broken hearts?" Jack protested. "Get your ass back here and listen to him."

"I've been single as long as you have," Cade said as the elevator opened and a pair of twenty-something twins walked out, eyeing him as if he'd said the magic word—*single*.

He focused on the wall straight in front of him. While that label still applied—and would for as long as he served in the Navy—this weekend he was attached to the woman he'd met last night. But he had a feeling "midfantasy fling" wasn't a tried-and-true relationship term.

"But you've managed your dad's broken heart for years," Jack pointed out.

"Yeah, I'm a freaking expert on how military life wrecks marriages," Cade said with disgust. "And speaking of my dad, I'm late to meet him."

"Taking a break from Natalie's sister?" his teammate teased.

"She's at the spa." *Letting some stranger rub oil over her naked body.*

With that mental image flashing in his mind, he glanced at the hall, tempted to march up to the desk and demand to know if a man or woman had been assigned to Lucia. The thought of another man running his hands over her...

He stepped away from the elevators. He shouldn't care. After tomorrow, she could play the fantasy sex game with anyone she wanted.

Fuck me, I'm going to spend the next month, possibly longer, wondering who's touching her.

His grip tightened on the phone. It was too late to avoid that particular hell.

"Natalie told me that if I talked to you, I should tell you to behave yourself," Jack said. "So I have to ask, as your friend and one of the people responsible for saving your ass most of the time, are you getting into trouble?"

"I'm going to spend the next hour or so listening to my dad bitch about his failed marriage. If you ask me, I could use a little trouble."

Just wait until I get to the Post-it note part of the evening.

"And a beer," his teammate added.

"Well, I'm meeting my father at a bar, so I'll take your advice. Go back inside, Jack. Get Dante out of there before he does something stupid."

"I think that ship has sailed," Jack said with a sigh.

Yeah, and I'm on it right beside Dante. Hell, if I follow those diagrams I drew for her on the beach, I deserve to be the captain of the damn vessel.

"I'm looking through the window," Jack continued. "And I think our man just handed his phone to Natalie. And we both know he's not showing her pictures from our latest mission."

Cade closed his eyes, part of him glad he wasn't in Coronado right now. "Get in there. Confiscate his phone if you have to."

"I'm going," Jack said. "You know the worst part of this mess? Natalie will blame me. She always does."

Get in line.

Cade ended the call and got on the elevator. Jack was right. Cade had a window into Dante's situation. As far as Cade knew, his mother had never had an affair. But he'd watched loneliness eat at her day after day. In the end, his mother had decided she couldn't be married to a man who put his job first. And his father had refused to retire while he still had the strength and willpower to serve. The divorce papers labeled it "irreconcilable differences," but Cade knew those differences could be summed up in one word—Navy.

At the end of the day, Cade admired the hell out of both his parents for being true to themselves. He just wished he hadn't been caught in the crosshairs. First, living with his mother's pain. And later, listening to his father mourn the relationship he'd given all he had to give to—even though it wasn't enough.

And now his teammate had learned the same lesson. Their commitment to the teams didn't leave enough space for anyone else.

The elevator door opened, and Cade headed for the bar by the casino floor. Set back behind velvet ropes, the place wasn't exactly quiet. But it served decent beer on tap and would suit his father a helluva lot more than the hotel's fancy wine bar. And it showed baseball on multiple flat-screen TVs.

He spotted his father, Calvin Daniels, perched on a leather bar stool. After twenty-two years in the Navy, fifteen spent with the SEALs, his father's face had a weathered look. But he was otherwise in good shape. He kept his gray hair military-short and stayed fit by running and lifting weights. Cade figured his dad could probably bench almost as much as he could. Almost.

"Hey, Dad, thanks for driving over to the Strip to meet me." He slapped his dad on the back as he claimed the stool beside him.

His father's go-to serious expression broke into a megawatt smile. "I'm glad you could find some time for your old man."

"After tomorrow, I'm all yours for a few days," Cade said. "But I need to head back to Coronado by Thursday. I'm saving the rest of my leave for the holidays."

"Heading out to see your mom this year?"

"For Thanksgiving if I can," Cade confirmed, signaling the bartender. The petite, bright-eyed redhead behind the bar appeared to be about his age. The name tag affixed to her hotel uniform read Maxine. "I'll take a pale ale, whatever you have on draft."

As Maxine moved to the taps, her ringlets bouncing, Cade glanced at his dad.

The retired SEAL looked away from the game and turned to him. "Have you talked to your mom recently?"

"I spoke with her when I got back to Coronado," he said, accepting the beer with a nod. "She's good. Happy."

"With Rhett." His dad spit out Cade's stepfather's name. "I can't understand why she didn't wait. I was so close to retirement. Being a SEAL is a young man's game, you know that."

"Yeah, but I think Mom worried that even if you retired

after serving your twenty years, you'd sit around and sulk, missing the Navy."

And that's exactly what happened, except I'm the one who has to listen to you.

"If she'd moved closer to Coronado, become part of that tight-knit community, she'd have been okay," his dad said. "She needed people around her who understood."

"Maybe." *But maybe she just needed you.*

His dad took a long drink from his beer. "It's a hard thing, son. Telling the woman you love that there's something more important in your life. And that you're standing by your duty to serve your country until your body gives out. Hell, I would have stayed past the twenty-two-year mark if my knees hadn't quit on me."

"I know."

His dad went on as if Cade hadn't said a word. "If your mom had been around other families, women she could turn to with her fears, I think things would have been different. For all of us."

It was an old argument. Cade could still picture his parents fighting over the dining room table on the rare days his dad was home. His mother would counter with the fact that she'd rather spend the months he was deployed surrounded by family and friends, not other struggling military wives.

"That doesn't always make it better," Cade said, thinking of Dante drunk in a bar sharing his wife's sexting exploits with anyone who would listen. Dante had made sure his wife had every opportunity to interact with the other wives and girlfriends. And his teammate was still likely heading for the big D.

"Most of the guys on my teams had wives waiting for them back home," his dad added.

"And how many are still married?" Cade challenged.

"About half," his father admitted, then drained his beer.

He signaled the bartender for a refill. "Enough about me."

Thank God.

"Tell me what you're doing on the Strip, anyway."

"A friend got me into a restaurant opening," he said. His dad didn't need to know why Natalie had sent him, but he couldn't just leave it at that. "I met this woman there. She's gorgeous. And we're in the same boat, looking for a break from the everyday. Nothing more."

"You just spent, what, six months overseas?"

Cade nodded. "And this time, the things we saw…it wasn't pretty."

"It never is." His dad slapped him on the back. "You need a little fun before you go back to your team. Blow off a little steam. She sounds perfect. So where's this gorgeous girl now?"

"I dropped her at the spa, called in a favor from Mom's friend Anna. Remember her?"

His dad's brow furrowed. "Yeah, she never liked me."

"Well, she hooked me up with an afternoon of pampering. Lucia's life back home isn't sunshine and roses," Cade said. "I want her to feel special for a couple of days."

"You're seeing her again tonight?" his dad asked.

"Yes, but she leaves tomorrow."

And after that I'll never see her again. This is my last chance to make her feel beautiful.

His father smiled at the bartender. "Darling, what's the hottest restaurant in Vegas?"

"Chef Louis's new place." She frowned. "But it books up months in advance."

His father leaned forward. "My son's a Navy SEAL—"

"Dad," Cade said. "I'm sure there's someplace else we can go." He didn't advertise his job, and he sure as hell didn't use it to secure reservations. His old man should know better.

His father ignored him. "My son wants to spend his few days of leave making his girl feel like a princess. Spa treatments, fancy food, the whole nine yards."

True, but—

Across the bar, Maxine sighed, her lips forming a wistful smile. "I'll see what I can do."

"Thanks, Maxine." His dad turned to him as the bartender headed for the landline phone by the register. "Now, son, what are you planning to wear for your final night out with this special girl?"

Cade sipped his beer. "I brought clothes with me."

"A suit? To take a girl out to the hottest ticket in town, you need to look sharp."

This coming from the man who'd never expressed an interest in Cade's clothing choices growing up. Or his own apart from the desire to wear a uniform.

"I don't own a suit," Cade said flatly.

"After Maxine confirms your reservation, we'll hit the mall across the street. Do a little shopping."

Cade raised an eyebrow. "You want to ditch the baseball game to go to the mall?"

"One thing I learned in the Navy," his dad said. "You need to make every moment count."

Chapter Thirteen

"If what happens in Vegas stays in Vegas, I need to move here," Lucia murmured as her masseuse lifted the lavender eye mask off her face. She blinked and opened her eyes to the dimly lit treatment room.

The woman laughed as she adjusted the rubber band containing her brown curls in a messy ponytail. "I'm glad you enjoyed the massage. Please take your time getting up. And just in case you decide to move to this crazy patch of desert, I'll leave my card beside your glass of water. Or you can just ask for Karen the next time you visit our spa."

The young woman set a business card on the side table and smiled before slipping out of the room. Lucia closed her eyes, determined to remain in her relaxed cocoon for a few more minutes.

"Sex in the ice room, followed by a massage," she murmured. "This is the best day ever."

The shrill ring of her cell cut into her bliss. She sat up, reluctantly slid off the table, and retrieved her phone from her robe.

"Natalie, I'm in heaven and you're interrupting," she said, lying back on the table.

"Right now?" The note of hysteria in his sister's voice caught her by surprise. "You're with him *now* and you answered the phone?"

"Not sex heaven," Lucia corrected. "Massage heaven. I'm in a treatment room at the hotel's spa. Cade, the guy I met last night, the Navy SEAL, he arranged for a ninety-minute hot-stone massage."

"He took you to a spa?" Disbelief replaced her sister's frenzied panic, but she still sounded off.

"He's perfect," Lucia declared with a sigh.

"I seriously doubt that."

She grinned. There was the sarcastic sister she knew and loved.

"If you're calling to check on me, you can stop worrying," Lucia said, sitting up and reaching for the water.

"You flew across the country to meet a stranger," her sister shot back. "Someone needs to worry about you. And if you refuse to do it, I will. What happens if this guy isn't as great as he appears?"

"Natalie, I'm in control." Holding the phone against her ear with her shoulder, she slid one arm into the robe. "That's your secret to life, right? Controlling everything?"

The bitter words felt out of place in the serene treatment room. Lucia closed her eyes and took a deep breath. Natalie loved her. But they looked at the world through different eyes.

Natalie had struggled with handing over control to their foster families, rebelling against the idea that strangers should have a say in her life. But Lucia had hoped to find acceptance. And instead had been marked worthless.

"I'm in control," Lucia insisted. *Of finding a way to feel wanted for one weekend.*

"How do you know you can control a man you just met?"

Natalie demanded. "And he's a SEAL. You can't manage guys like him. Believe me, I see them every day. In fact, I just kicked a pair of drunken SEALs out of my bar."

Lucia laughed. "I think I found a way."

"I'm serious—"

"So am I," she said, setting aside the mental picture of Cade's wrists bound above his head. The restraint had only offered the illusion of control over him. His desire to be a part of her dreams for this weekend had paved the way for trust. Every touch, every kiss, every naughty word that crossed his lips, every orgasm proved that the wanting ran both ways. If he'd just wanted sex, he would have walked away already. He wanted *her*.

Sure, she dreamed of a guy who'd treat her that way for longer than a weekend. But Cade had been clear he wasn't that kind of guy. That she'd be disappointed even if he tried to be. She just hoped she wouldn't be too heartbroken when it came time to tell him good-bye.

"Natalie, I've been bold and daring for a long time on a canvas," she said, pulling the robe on the rest of the way and securing the belt. "But here, with Cade, I'm brave without needing to rely on my paintbrush. And I love feeling like I don't have to hide."

"I don't want to see you get hurt," Natalie said. "Ever."

"I'm a big girl. This is just a fling. I told him that from the start."

A knock sounded at the door. "Just checking to see if you fell asleep," Karen called through the door. "It happens sometimes."

"I'll be right out," Lucia promised the masseuse. Dropping her voice low, she added, "Natalie, I need to go. But I promise, I'll text you in the morning."

A dog barked in the background. And Lucia would've sworn she heard her sister mutter, "I'm going to kill him," just before the line cut out.

She slipped her phone into one of the robe's front pockets, and then she headed for the door. She'd meant what she said to Natalie. This was her chance to be bold. And the next stop was the salon.

. . .

"Close your eyes."

Cade heard Lucia's voice through the hotel room door. His hands froze on the zipper of his new dress pants. He'd left the rental tux with the concierge after he'd moved his duffel into Lucia's suite that morning. And his dad was right—he needed a step up from jeans or board shorts for tonight.

So after six months deployed to a war-torn country, he'd spent the afternoon shopping with his dad while his date for the evening visited the spa. When he'd walked back into normal, everyday life, it felt like the twilight zone.

"Are they closed?" The sound of a key card unlocking the door followed her words.

"Yes." He was standing by the bed, his pants still undone, his new shirt hanging in the closet, and a present for his date on the desk. His hands moved to his sides, and his eyelids drifted shut.

"Don't peek," she warned as the door slammed shut behind her. "Okay, now you can look."

He opened his eyes and turned around. Her long hair tumbled over her shoulders, and her big, loose curls drew his gaze down to her chest.

"Anna, your friend at the salon, called it the Sofia Vergara special. Have you heard of her?"

"Yes." He'd watched the actress's popular sitcom with Natalie. And Sofia Vergara's hair was only one of her many attributes he'd admired. But the sitcom beauty came in a distant second to Lucia.

For years, he'd played by the rules he'd written for himself since he joined the Navy—nothing serious. He'd never invested beyond a night or two. And in return, whatever emotions or insecurities might have come to the surface instead remained locked away.

But Lucia had let him in. Even before the mask came off, she'd given him glimpses into what drove her passions in bed and out. And after the mask fell, she'd let him see her. The *real* her.

"Cade," she asked, her brow furrowed. "What do you think?"

"I think it's a damn shame you have to wear a dress to dinner. I'd rather see your curls teasing your bare breasts all night."

She rewarded him with a sensual smile. "We could order room service."

"No, I'm taking you out." He walked over to the minibar and pulled out a bottle of bourbon. He needed to feel something other than the unnerving need to strip off her clothes and take her. Nothing kinky. Just plain old missionary, his body hovering over hers, offering him a clear view of her face as he took her.

Claim her.

Except she wasn't his. And after tonight, she would slip out of his life. There was no way around it. Hell, he'd been trained to think outside the box, but he couldn't find a path forward that didn't involve hurting her.

If he tried for more, she'd discover he'd been on a mission to find her that first night. And if that didn't break the woman fighting for a way forward, crawling out from under a past that had taken too damn much, the fact that a relationship with him would lead to loneliness just might crush her.

He unscrewed the top to the miniature bottle and sat

down on a corner of the bed. "Put on your dress," he said.

She raised an eyebrow, and he lifted his gaze to the makeup on her face. Anna had kept it simple, allowing Lucia's big brown eyes to shine. And her red lips were a masterpiece, shifting attention away from her cheek to the mouth that featured heavily in his fantasies. He owed his mother's friend a thank-you call for going all in.

"You're just going to sit there and watch?" she asked.

"Yes." He raised the bottle to his lips and took a drink. "I want to walk out of this room hard for you. While we're out, I'll be counting down the minutes until we return."

She turned her back to him and slipped her black cover-up over her head, revealing her black one-piece suit. "Where are we going?"

"A supper club with a reputation for creative drinks, good food, and live entertainment." He tracked her movements as she drew the straps down her shoulders.

"You've been?" She opened the closet door.

"No. The bartender at the place where I met my dad recommended it."

The suit still covering her, she disappeared behind the door. "How was your afternoon with your father?"

"Better than expected," he admitted. "He was the one who quizzed the bartender on the hot new places in Vegas. And convinced her to secure our reservation."

"Your dad planned our night?"

"Yeah. And it was a nice change of pace. Most of the time when I see him, he rehashes the past over and over." Cade took another drink of bourbon. "Now that the tables are turned and he's the one left alone, I think he feels guilty for the way things worked out with my mom. She was always complaining about the waiting. And my dad didn't get it."

"Get what?" she asked.

"The Navy and relationships don't mix. My parents are

proof of that."

"Do you visit him often?" She reached out and tossed her suit onto the floor beside the mirror.

"No. I'm deployed or training most of the time. Last year, I spent over three hundred days outside the U.S. And I try to see my mom some, too." He leaned forward and rested his forearms on his thighs. Knowing the woman who drove him insane with a need that bordered on wild stood behind that mirror…shit, his parents were damn near close to the last thing he wanted to think about right now.

"What's wrong?" she said.

"I can't see you."

"I know." She leaned her head out and wrapped her fingers around the closet door's edge. "I've never done this before. But I want to be bold. And I want to give you a very private Vegas show."

Oh, fuck yeah.

"Please," he growled. "Do it."

He held his breath as she stepped out from behind the mirror. A slip of black lace dangled from her fingers. His gaze roamed over every naked inch of her body as she leaned down and her breasts fell forward. She stepped one foot into her panties, then the second. Slowly, she curled up and drew the black lace over her calves up to her thighs.

His hands tightened around the bottle to keep from reaching for her. So he'd translated Natalie's ultimatum—*the clothes stay on*—into the clothes going back on. He wasn't touching. Or tasting. Not yet.

But later, when they returned to the room, he planned to prove how much he desired every inch of her beautiful body. He'd save his regrets for daylight. And he'd keep them out of her reach. Tonight, he would hand this goddess one undeniable truth.

"You're beautiful," he said as she pulled the thong into

place and reached for her dress. "If you don't feel like a goddess, I promise you will by the time the sun rises."

"But tonight we're following your Post-its." Her red lips formed a playful smile. And her eyes sparkled with a hint of mischief as she turned her back to him. Slowly, she pulled the dress over her head.

"All night I'm going to be picturing what's beneath your clothes," he said. "Knowing that I'm the only man in the room who can name the color of your panties."

Her hands stilled, the fabric bunched at her waist. "Most people don't look at me and wonder about my underwear."

With her back to him, he couldn't read her expression. But he had a feeling doubt had extinguished her playful smile. And it threatened to throw the brakes on daring and bold.

"I'd bet about half the men at the restaurant tonight take one look at you and think how it would feel to fuck your breasts," he said. "And I'm the lucky bastard who plans to find out."

She let out a sharp laugh. "Just say the word and we can tackle fantasy number one right now."

Yes.

Little Miss Temptation threatened to ruin his strategy for the evening. But he'd been trained to tackle hurdles when it came to getting from point A to point B.

"Put your dress on," he said. "I'm taking you out first."

She shimmied her hips—a move that spoke directly to his dick—and pulled the dress on. The undone zipper left her back and her thong exposed. He savored each second before she pulled up the zipper, but she surprised him and first bent over to slip her black heels onto her feet.

"I fucking love it when you're bold." He leaned back, the bottle in one hand as the other pressed against the erection threatening to break free from his new pants.

"I'm glad you like the view," she murmured, securing the

ribbons around her ankles. But her tone distracted him from her movements. He'd expected flirtatious, but she'd said those words with an honesty that cut into him. If he called her over, he could have her on the bed, her dress bunched at her waist while he showed her just what the view did to him.

"I like *you*. In bed and out." He drew his hand away from his crotch and stood. "I'll get ready, and then we'll head out."

He walked into the bathroom and pulled the door shut behind him. Marble covered every surface in the space. His bedroom in Coronado would fit inside this room. He placed his hands on the edge of the matching sinks and stared into the mirror.

Over and over, he'd played the altruistic card.

This is for her.

Make her feel beautiful.

But he was in this for himself, too. And the sex was only one piece of the picture. He had a job that demanded his all, and he gave it. Teammates, friends, family on both coasts, and a dog waited for him in Coronado. His life was far from empty.

Yet right now he couldn't escape the loneliness. He'd found it easy to ignore, at least until this weekend. Until Lucia.

One more night in Sin City with a woman who left him wanting beyond reason. That's all it could be. His job would eventually take all he had to give and then some.

Chapter Fourteen

"Which door will you choose?" The hostess's words echoed in the empty, quiet hallway.

If someone had told Lucia earlier that one of the hottest new restaurants on the Strip was literally hidden like an old fashioned speakeasy, she would have laughed. She'd tried to bite back a giggle during their third elevator ride to find the place. But Cade's remark—*I've had an easier time finding terrorist cells*—had pushed her over the edge.

Now that they'd arrived, she watched the hostess turn in a semicircle and gesture to the six sets of nondescript double doors. The woman's long black dress draped over her tall, slim figure, a departure from the typical short-and-tight Vegas uniform. And her wild mane of tight blond curls combined with her dramatic, dark makeup took the look to the far side of eccentric.

"Do they all lead to food?" Cade asked, his fingers toying with the gift bag's handle. He'd sparked her curiosity earlier when he'd plucked it off the desk in the hotel room.

"Yes," the crazy-haired woman said. "But each room

offers a different experience designed to tease and tantalize. Which one will you choose?"

The door that leads to a private place where my date can slide his cock between my breasts?

She bit her lower lip before the words slipped out. On any other night, Vegas's hot new restaurant's creative spin on the whole dining experience might be fun. But tonight, Cade's long, thick length was the only thing she wanted teasing her. The way he'd watched her, the sound of his voice—her Navy SEAL transformed anticipation into an art.

He wrapped an arm around her waist and drew her close. "If I'd known dinner came with surprises, I would have chosen someplace else. But we're here now. And if we want to eat, we have to choose. It's your call."

She pushed the erotic images to the back of her mind and focused on the doors. If the man who'd spent the past twenty-four hours making her wildest dreams come true— the man who listened when she told him she didn't like the unexpected—wanted to take her out to dinner, she would do her part and pick a door.

"Number three," she said.

"Excellent choice," the hostess declared as she marched up to the double doors and pulled them open.

With Cade's arm tight around her, she followed the wild-haired woman into the dimly lit room. Hardwood tables surrounded by plush benches and chairs filled the railroad-style space. Works of art lined the walls, a mix of portraits and abstracts. The paintings were well lit, and candles offered the only lighting on the dining tables.

"Welcome to the gallery," the hostess said.

"It's perfect," Lucia murmured.

"This is one of my favorites," the woman confided. "But it's not as popular as the others."

"Most of your patrons dislike number three?" Cade

asked mildly.

"Visitors tend to read the reviews online and decide which door to pick. The owners initially wanted to rotate the spaces, but the financial backers balked at the expense. We were already over budget on the decor and the talent." The hostess shook her head as they wove through the tables to a counter booth. "It's a shame, really. It would have added to the experience."

"I should have offered to paint for the people who created this place," Lucia murmured, scanning the series of portraits and abstract paintings lining the walls. "They sound just crazy enough to pay a fortune."

The hostess stopped in front of a velvet love seat tucked into a corner. A table lined with candles stood in front of it. Couples were seated on two-tops with settees in the other corners.

"Your waiter will be over with your menus," the hostess said before disappearing into the dark room.

"You were right," Lucia said, sliding into a booth. "It was worth leaving the room for this experience."

A spotlight cut through the space illuminating a ring lowering from the pressed-tin ceiling. Cade sat down beside her and pressed his thigh up against her leg as a woman in a nude leotard began moving. With her hands holding tight to the bottom of the ring, the acrobat flipped her legs over her head and arched her back until her toes touched her forehead.

"Impressive," Cade said.

A young man who looked as if he'd dressed for the Mad Hatter's tea party in his oversize suit and top hat stopped in front of their table and held out menus. "The top one lists our signature cocktails and the bottom is our food menu. May I offer you still or sparkling water?"

He glanced at Lucia. "You first."

"Still. And a champagne cocktail." She quickly scanned

the list. "This first one here. The Dancer's Dream."

"I'll have an old-fashioned," he said without glancing at the menu.

The waiter nodded and disappeared into the darkness. She stole one more glance at the woman transforming herself into a pretzel fifteen feet in the air, then turned to Cade. "You are old-fashioned, aren't you?" she teased. "Insisting on a dinner date."

"If we'd stayed in the room, I would have my hands on your breasts right now." He leaned close and brushed the hair off her shoulder. His index finger ran down her neck, igniting her nerves. Beneath her dress, her nipples tightened, adding a touch-me-now plea to the conversation.

"While that sounds satisfying…" he continued, his finger tracing her collarbone, "I promised to show you the sights and sounds of Vegas beyond your hotel room. And if that means I need to endure a few hours staring at your gorgeous body barely hidden by that dress, knowing I'm going to own it later, I'm in."

"You take your promises seriously," she murmured.

He withdrew his hand and caressed her cheek. "I do my best."

"Me too." She placed one hand on his thigh and touched her lips to his ear. "What if I promised to take the edge off your suspense?"

His muscles tightened beneath her fingers, propelling her courage forward. This man had teased her from the moment they met. Here, in the dark corner of the restaurant, she wanted to give him something in return.

"Have you had a chance to look at the menu?" the waiter interrupted, placing their cocktails on the table.

"We need more time," Cade said, the words hard and sharp.

"A lot more time," Lucia added, sitting up straight. She

kept her hand on Cade's leg and reached for a sip of liquid courage with the other.

The waiter nodded and retreated into the semidarkness.

Cade turned to Lucia, a question mark clear and present in his furrowed brow. "Planning to offer me a peek beneath your dress before the waiter returns?"

"Not exactly." She moved her hand up and down his thigh. "But I know how anticipation can eat away at you. For example, I'm dying to know what's in the gift bag."

"Something I saw this afternoon that made me think of you," he said. "I'll let you open it now if you tell me how you plan to take the edge off."

She laughed. "You don't like surprises either, do you?"

"I try to avoid them whenever possible. Most of the ones I face tend to end badly," he admitted. "I can be patient when I need to be. But if there's a way to learn what I want to know, I'll take it."

"Deal." She set her drink down and held out her hand. "The bag, please."

He picked up the plain white gift bag overflowing with red tissue paper and held it out. She peered inside and tried to catch a glimpse at her present before she tore the paper out.

"Now you're willing to let anticipation linger?" he said.

"It's been a long time since anyone has given me a present." She reached for the tissue paper lining the top of the bag. "Last Valentine's Day, the kids I was working with at the time made beaded necklaces for me."

"I didn't buy you jewelry," he said, his tone reassuring, as if he knew she secretly craved something unique that spoke to her.

She reached into the tissue paper…and found a long rectangular box. She pulled it free and stared at her present. "You bought me a watercolor set."

"There's a sketchbook in there, too," he added. "Last

night, by the fountains, you mentioned wanting to paint what you saw."

"Thank you." She took out the sketchbook and set it beside the paints on the table. She flipped open the watercolors, then picked up the slim brush inside and dipped it in her water glass. In another restaurant, she'd probably draw disapproving looks from the staff. But she had a feeling their Mad Hatter server wouldn't blink an eye.

"I'm glad you're excited to get started," Cade said. "But I think you're forgetting your side of the bargain."

"Now's the time to be patient." She swirled the wet brush through the black paint. "I'd like to do a before and after series."

He leaned back against the love seat's red velvet and studied the room. "You want to paint the girl in the ring before she finishes her act?"

"No, I'm painting you," she murmured, focusing on the lines of his face.

He raised an eyebrow. "Before and after what?"

She studied his face, noting the way he schooled his expression. On the surface, she saw his curiosity and desire, but beyond that, there was so much more. He'd given her a glimpse when he spoke of his dedication to the Navy and his haunted past with his parents.

Her hand moved over the paper, translating what she saw into shapes and lines. Adding shades of color to the black outline.

"Do you always paint people?" he asked, turning his gaze to the performance near the ceiling.

"No, most of my work resembles the paintings you saw at the opening last night. But I still do the occasional portrait." She dipped her brush in the water again, touched it to the paints and then the paper.

"Why did you choose to paint abstracts instead of

portraits?" he asked.

"When my therapist first introduced the idea of using art to express what I was feeling, she told me to create a self-portrait. But when I thought about painting myself, I didn't see lines," she continued, focused on the paper in front of her. "Or a face. I saw colors. Later, I realized I was painting what I felt."

"The colors represent your emotions?"

In her peripheral vision, she saw him lift his glass to his lips.

"In a way," she said. "Although it's not as simple as anger equals red. Sometimes there isn't a linear path between words and emotions. Especially for kids. And many times, a grown-up's idea of how to process trauma or change doesn't work for a child. Adults have grown accustomed to using their words. But kids, even teenagers on the cusp of adulthood, often need a different outlet. Painting, drawing, a physical expression of what is happening inside helps them process the world around them."

"I've seen a lot of kids who could use your help," he said.

"I can imagine," she murmured.

"There was this one kid. Nine or ten. I'm not great with ages, and this boy had probably spent months, maybe years, struggling with hunger. But he'd found a stick and was drawing in the dirt. What stuck with me, the reason I did a double take while we were moving through the area, was that this kid wasn't just passing the time. He drew with purpose and determination."

He lifted one hand and ran it through his hair, pressing his eyes closed for a split second, as if locking the memory away in the vault.

No wonder he wants to escape his past and everything that makes him who he is for a few fantasy-filled nights. This man has witnessed nightmares.

The waiter returned and asked, "Ready to order? Questions about the menu?"

Cade's relief permeated their intimate space as he reached for the menu. After they ordered, the waiter disappeared. The spotlight turned on again, this time illuminating a piano in the corner to the right of their table. A man wearing a tuxedo with the tails draped over the bench began to play a classical piece that sounded vaguely familiar.

"Have you finished painting?" Cade asked.

Lucia nodded, glancing down at the portrait. The man in the picture looked lonely. She picked up the brush and swirled it in one color after another, creating a frenzied background layered with pinks, reds, greens, and blues. She set the brush down and glanced at the paper. This was what she saw when she looked at Cade—a man who promised to give to the people around him but remained closed off to taking for himself.

But now it was her turn to give.

"All done." She set the painting on the far side of the table to dry. She slipped her left hand under the long tablecloth and touched his thigh. "You've been very patient."

"I liked watching you paint," he said.

"You'll like this more," she promised.

She ran her hand up to his crotch and moved her palm up and down, mapping the shape of his long, hard length. He locked his gaze with hers and raised one of his eyebrows. Her fingers moved to his zipper, drew it down. His eyes widened as she slipped her hand inside and freed his cock from his boxer briefs.

She stole a look around the restaurant. No one was looking at them. The other diners were focused on themselves or the lingerie-clad tap dancers who'd just stepped onto the stage beside the man seated at the piano.

She began to stroke him. "Tell me what you want," she

said. "How you like to be touched."

"Lucia." The raspy quality of his deep voice betrayed his desire.

She turned her body toward him, reached her free arm under the table, and cupped his balls with her right hand. He groaned and lifted his hips off the love seat.

The sight of the big, bad Navy SEAL demanding more from her touch left her bold, determined, and wondering if she should slip her hand under her dress and roll her fingers over her clit. But no, this was for him.

"This wasn't on my list," he said as she stroked him harder and faster.

One of the lingerie-clad tap dancers sped up, the sound of her shoes threatening to drown out the piano.

But Cade wasn't looking at the show. His eyes roamed over Lucia as if they were the only two people in the room—and she was all he needed to come hard and fast under the table.

"Tell me what you want," she demanded. "Because I'm adding 'give Cade a hand job in a restaurant' to mine."

Chapter Fifteen

She does a helluva lot better job at keeping her promises than I do.

Cade had gone from swearing to do the right thing and keep his hands off his best friend's sister to letting her jerk him off before the waiter returned with their meal.

Technically, the clothes had stayed on. But if they got arrested for this, word would probably get back to Natalie. His best friend would go after his balls with the small, dull knife she used to cut lemons behind the bar. And he could forget about seeing his dog again.

He should tell Lucia to stop. Just like he should have told her he'd been sent to watch out for her. She deserved to know the truth.

She slowed her hand near the tip of his dick and swept her thumb through the liquid that beaded up. He groaned. Hell, she deserved a gold medal in hand jobs.

"You like that?" she murmured. Her full, red lips curled into a mischievous smile he swore was designed to work alongside her touch, pushing him closer to the finish line.

"Yes," he gasped. And she repeated the movement. But he needed more.

"What else? Just tell me what you need," she said.

"Tight and fast." His hand covered hers, showing her how to send their little trip to fantasyland barreling toward the goal line.

She grinned, a signal that she understood his instructions, so he released her hand and pressed his palm into the love seat. He looked around the room, half expecting to find wide-eyed stares. Maybe the hostess heading for their table, ready to kick them out.

But no one was looking at them. The other guests appeared enthralled with the frantic music coming from the piano.

Then Lucia's other hand teased his balls and the rest of the room faded away. His gaze locked on hers. He'd witnessed her shy and embarrassed. He'd seen her tumble into pleasure. And he'd studied her near-orgasmic expression while she ate a piece of chocolate. But the look in her eyes right now threatened to do him in.

"Does it turn you on?" she asked. "Knowing all these people are nearby while I have your cock in my hand?"

"No." It was by the grace of the crazy women causing a racket beside the piano that no one had glanced over at them. "It's not them." He reached his right hand up, wove his fingers through her salon-perfect hair, and drew her mouth to his. "It's the wild, fun, beautiful woman sitting next to me."

His tongue swept inside her mouth. She let out a soft moan. He might be holding back the truth, but when it came to his actions, he swore he'd give her everything he had.

Her hand tightened around him, stroking faster.

He grabbed a napkin off the table and quickly covered his lap. "Don't stop. I'm going to come."

Because one glance at her and he saw a bold, daring woman who knew what she wanted—him.

And he came so hard that all he could utter was a strangled gasp of pleasure.

He allowed the rush to wash over him and fade away. He'd been on covert missions that dialed the adrenaline up to one hundred, but this felt like the biggest damn thrill of his life.

He gently moved her hand away and went to work cleaning up and putting his very grateful dick back in his pants. She grinned as if she'd walked into dinner expecting to make him come under the table. Shit, maybe she had. Beneath her insecurities, she was the woman he'd met at the opening. A little brazen, and fun to the point that it was intoxicating.

"Looks like we finished just in time," she said with a nod to the approaching server.

The man in the strange suit dropped off their entrees, then returned moments later with a clean glass of water. Lucia pushed her steaming plate away and reached for her paints.

"Not hungry?" Cade said.

"I need to paint your after portrait." She flipped to a fresh page in the sketchbook he'd bought for her and dipped her brush in the clean water.

"You don't want to eat first?" he asked. "While it's hot?"

She shook her head, her attention on the paper. "I want to capture the way you look right now."

"Satisfied?"

She looked up at him from underneath her long lashes. "You look like a man who wants more."

His smile faded as he cut into his steak. Between the hand job and those words, she'd pushed him off his axis tonight.

For so long, his life had been a series of missions. No girlfriends. No connections he couldn't leave behind when the call came in to deploy. Sure, he had his dad. But his old man understood. And his mother had shifted her focus to her new life, closing herself off to the pain of having a loved one in harm's way most of the year. Right now, his biggest commitment was to his dog. And he had joint custody that felt more like visitation with each deployment.

Hell, maybe he did want more. But every time he tried to put the pieces together in his head, they delivered him to his dad's not so happy ever after.

Cade stabbed his steak as Lucia bent over the sketchbook. A long band of hair fell across her good cheek, and her body leaned forward as if every inch of her was invested in her creation. It was fucking mesmerizing. How the hell was he going to walk away from her?

You don't have to. Not yet.

"I do want more," he said.

She looked up at the sound of his voice, her brown eyes widening.

"I want to see your dress hit the floor," he continued. "The minute we step inside your room, I want you naked on the bed. And tonight, I plan to work through every fantasy on my list."

Lucia focused on the paper, trying to mask her disappointment. When he'd said those words—*I do want more*—her hope had surged. The fantasy would follow her home, bringing the best piece of her Vegas vacation back to her day-to-day life.

Except that wasn't what he'd meant.

She could walk away from the fancy restaurants and the breathtaking fountains. She'd survive with the memory of little umbrellas in her drinks. But she couldn't ignore her desire to keep Cade in her life.

And in the moments after his orgasm, he'd looked like he wanted it, too. He'd kissed her as if he needed to claim parts of her body, to feel connected to her while she touched him under the table.

But more wasn't part of the plan. Not beyond their sexual connection. Not beyond this weekend. She should know. She'd set the rules from the beginning. This ended tomorrow when she returned to Tennessee.

"I'd better get to work on this portrait." Her hand moved quickly, painting the after look from memory. The man tearing into his steak as if he hadn't eaten in days had already drawn up his defenses, blocking her out again.

She cocked her head, studying the incomplete picture. The lines and colors looked right, but something was missing. She touched the brush to the paper and tried again.

"You're talented." His low voice splintered her focus, and she lifted the brush off the page. "I can't believe you're doing all of that with a set of watercolors from the Vegas mall. I was serious when I asked to see the rest of your work."

"I have a few pictures on my phone." She set the brush down, reached into her purse, and withdrew her cell. She entered the pass code and clicked on the photo icon. "You're welcome to scroll through them."

She returned her attention to her current work-in-progress. Something was off. The image failed to convey emotion.

She bit her lower lip. Maybe the piece wasn't working because she wanted to portray a feeling that hadn't been part of the scene in the first place. He'd had an orgasm, not an epiphany that opened his eyes to a new future—one that included her.

She set the brush on the table, leaving the painting incomplete, and reached for her dinner.

"Maybe I'll get to see the real thing one day," he said, still paging through the images on her phone.

A shiver ran through her, every inch of her silently screaming, *yes, please.*

"Or maybe you'll let me keep one of the paintings from tonight," he added.

Not the disastrous after, she thought, letting her hope fade. "Maybe," she said softly.

He held out her cell. "When did you paint this one?"

She set the fork on her plate and pretended to take a closer look, even though she knew which one was on the screen. The light pastels, the vague illusions of silhouettes holding hands by the water—she'd recognize that piece anywhere.

"That's one of my first paintings. It still hangs in my studio where I can see it before I start my day, or while I'm working." She picked up her drink, downing the bubbly liquid in a few quick gulps.

Years ago, she'd struggled to create that image, too, scared to record what she felt versus what she wished to feel. But sometimes emotions were like mountains. She couldn't move and change them to suit the picture she wanted to create.

"Does this convey a single emotion?" he asked, focused on the small image that represented a huge piece of her life. "About what happened?"

Her hand went to her cheek. For a little while, her face had slipped into the background. She'd walked into a restaurant and sat through most of a meal without the jagged lines dictating her movements and reactions. "No, this piece isn't related to the incident or my scars."

He looked up, and his gaze met hers. And then he turned to his steak. Had he seen too much? Did one look leave him wondering if she wanted to rewrite the rules for their weekend?

"I'd been in therapy for months," she said quickly. "And I felt they were ignoring a large part of who I was. I began lashing out. And at one point, I refused to paint. Bethany, the therapist who introduced the idea of using art, insisted my feelings were linked to my foster father. So I painted this to show her that I was still heartbroken over the loss of my parents."

He nodded, his face etched with pity for the first time

since her mask had fallen off.

"Learning to live with what happened, with the scars on my face, is one thing, but facing a future without my mom and dad, that sometimes hurts just as much." She stared at the painting. Most days, she saw it when she stepped into her studio. "I was ten when they died. And I remember what it was like to feel wanted and loved unconditionally."

She waited for him to ask the usual questions. *How did they die? Did you have any other living relatives or family friends to take you in?* By now, she could talk about the car crash without dissolving into tears. She could explain that no, she had no other relatives besides Natalie. No aunts, no uncles. Even her grandmother had already been suffering from Alzheimer's when the crash happened.

"The shadows in the painting, those are your parents," he said.

"Yes."

"It's beautiful," he said, looking up from the picture as he held out her phone. "For all the grief I give my parents over the choices they made with their lives, I know I still have their love. I'm sorry for your loss."

"Thank you." She'd abandoned the seemingly obligatory "it was a long time ago" after she'd realized that she'd never stop mourning their abrupt end. Some days, she just plain wanted her family back. She missed that feeling of being loved and accepted, no matter what.

Maybe that was why the thought of saying good-bye to Cade felt so hard to endure. He made her feel like she was home again, and it would crush her when their weekend lease ran out.

What was she supposed to do? Just ask him to set aside his concerns and keep this thing going? He'd been clear how much he wanted and for how long. Who was she to think she deserved anything more?

He must have caught something in her expression, because he said, "I'm sorry. You didn't come to Vegas to talk about your past."

She shrugged. "You couldn't have known."

"Still. Let me make it up to you."

"Ready for dessert already?"

He held up his hand, signaling the server for the check. "I'd rather feast on you. And the box of chocolates I picked up earlier."

"The gifts just keep coming," she murmured as the server appeared with their bill. "Did you select ones that explode in your mouth?"

"We'll find out." He reached for his wallet.

"Let me pay for dinner," she said. "After everything you did today."

"No. Consider this the last piece of your Vegas tour."

After the server slipped away, he stood and held out his hand. He drew her up, leaned close, and in a quiet voice said, "When we get to your room, I want you to strip off your dress and climb on the bed. No robes tonight. Lie on your stomach and lift your hips just enough to run your hand between your legs. Drive yourself wild. And don't call for me until you're ready."

"I don't recall this Post-it drawing," she teased, his words pushing her close to calling out, *ready!*

He took her hand and led the way to a door marked EXIT. Heaven help her if this door led to another one of the rooms. She'd be tempted to strip off her dress in the library, the kitchen, or whatever space waited on the other side. And she'd probably land them both in trouble.

Two days ago, she'd been begging for a little bit of trouble. But now? Didn't she already have enough of that? Hell, she had more than she could handle. She was falling for a man who still planned to say good-bye tomorrow.

Chapter Sixteen

Time hovered like an enemy. But Cade felt powerless to stop the minutes, unlike his past foes, from slipping away as they drove down the Strip. And the elevator ride to their room lasted an eternity. If the confined space hadn't been filled with teenagers, he might have pushed her up against the elevator's mirrored interior and taken her.

But he'd bypassed the opportunity to see her pleasure reflected in the elevator mirrors. He wanted more than a quickie in the elevator. And now, finally, they were inside Lucia's suite, shut away from the rest of the world and the harsh realities waiting for them when the sun came up.

She set her bags down and reached for the zipper along the back of her dress. "Ready for your dreams to come true?"

You have no idea.

One look at her and he wished this fantasy could be their future. Days, nights, weeks, months sinking into her, kissing her. But outside this room, reality—the lies he'd told, the fact that he had to go back to work and likely ship out—would return.

"Please," he said, letting desire trump reason. "Let me see you."

To hell with fantasies, he needed her *now*.

Zipper undone, she shrugged out of the dress and abandoned the black fabric to the floor. Her underwear followed, and she climbed on the bed.

"Like this?" she asked, assuming the all-fours position he'd described in the restaurant.

Without taking his eyes off her, he walked toward her. "Perfect. So damn perfect."

Moving with a confidence that blew him away, she pressed her hands into the bedding and thrust her ass in the air.

"Are you sure? I think you described something more like this." She pressed the damaged side of her face against the bed. A teasing question floated in her brown eyes as her left hand drifted south.

"Yes," he growled.

He watched her hand slide over her bare skin and stripped off his new clothes. Her fingers disappeared inside then withdrew, offering proof she was wet and ready for him. Slowly, she slid her knees across the hotel blanket and opened her body to her touch, fingers moving faster and faster.

"Just like that," he murmured as he retrieved a condom and turned the foil packet over in his hand.

She lifted her head, and the movement sent her breasts gliding forward against the bedding. Her back arched at a nearly impossible angle. She rocked back and forth, her whole body moving against her hand.

His dick begged to climb up on the bed, rub up against her, and slip inside. He tore open the condom and rolled it over his erection.

"Do you want to watch me come? I'm close," she gasped, her face upturned. "Tell me what you want."

He placed one knee on the bed, but his gaze remained

fixed on her face. And the truth slammed into him.

He wanted to erase her past. From the beginning, he'd set out to prove her physical scars hadn't erased her beauty. He looked at her curves and saw a goddess. And her mouth? He couldn't imagine a day when he wouldn't want to thrust his dick between her full lips.

But they'd known from the beginning when this would end. The only way to even have a chance at something more meant revealing he'd betrayed her from the start. All the trust she'd given him shattered in an instant.

She'd already been betrayed by the people she trusted most. She had the scars to prove it. He wouldn't add to those scars. He wouldn't add to her pain.

Tomorrow, he'd walk away, his lies still intact. He'd send Lucia back to the children who needed her help while he returned to the one constant in his life—his team. By Tuesday morning, he would be nothing more than a memory. And by God, he'd make sure it was a good one.

"You deserve so much more than this," he said.

Her hand stilled. Lips parted, she stared at him, confusion etched into her expression.

"You should have someone who can give you more than a fantasy," he said, struggling to translate his feelings into words.

She deserved the type of no-holds-barred love that went hand in hand with commitment. But how the fuck could he say those words to her and tack on the fact that he couldn't be that man?

She smiled, and her hand returned to her clit.

Walking away from her, from this—there were parts of his body that might never forgive him. The thought of living with this image burned into his memory, knowing he'd turned his back on what came next—

"Cade," she said. "Tonight, I want to be the girl in *your*

fantasies. We can talk about tomorrow when the sun rises." She held his gaze in hers. "I've never felt this beautiful. This bold. Even without the mask, I feel wild."

Her hips moved faster and faster, pushing against her fingers. She let out a low moan as she withdrew her hand and drew a wet path over her stomach to her breasts. She paused there and teased her nipples before continuing up to her collarbone. Then she parted her lips and slipped her glistening fingers inside her mouth.

And that was all it took for him to let reason fall by the wayside.

"Fuck me," he murmured.

"I'm ready," she said. "And if you think I'm this wet because I want something more than your cock, you're crazy. Join me. And don't you dare hold anything back."

"You want to be the girl in my fantasies?" He took her face in his hands. "*You* are my fantasy."

He knew those words would hold true tomorrow and the day after that. Six months from now, deployed halfway around the world, he would wake up dreaming about this woman. And she would be out of his reach forever. Tonight was his only chance to make every moment count.

Lucia closed her eyes and pressed her hands into the mattress as Cade positioned himself at her entrance. In one fluid movement, he wrapped his hands around her hips and filled her.

She relished every piece of the sensation. The way she stretched to accommodate his long, thick length. The slap of his body against hers as he slid her forward on the bed with each thrust. The pinch of discomfort that bordered on pain as his fingers pressed into her hips and lifted her higher, adjusting her position to serve his needs.

His fingers bundled in her hair and gently pulled for her to turn her head toward him.

"Open your eyes," he said. "Look at me."

She obeyed, and the pieces of the puzzle fell together. The hard cock stretching her, the body pushing her closer and closer to a climax—each part of the picture belonged to the warrior behind her.

She pressed back, matched him stroke for stroke. She refused to let him own this moment alone. She wanted to give him something in return, to be a necessary part of this frenzied trip to his climax.

His hips moved faster and faster. If he released his hold on her, she'd slide into the headboard with his next powerful thrust.

"Tell me you're close," he demanded.

Just like that, the rough, raw edge to his panty-melting voice tipped her over the cliff marked with a giant, flashing *O*. Pleasure dominated her senses, owned her from head to toe.

He guided her down to the bed. Her knees splayed out and her hips sank into the mattress. He moved with her and lowered down on top of her as he continued to thrust.

"Gorgeous, you're so tight like this," he rasped. A low groan followed the words. His cock slid into her one last time and stayed there.

His ragged breathing filled the room. Beneath him, she wiggled her hips.

"Ah, hell, Lucia." She felt his chest lower down onto her back. "If you want more, I'll give it to you. Just say the word."

"More," she murmured. "More, more, *more*."

He rocked back, stealing away the intimate feel of his muscles blanketing her. "Roll over."

Mentally running through the positions on his list, she shifted to her back, her curious gaze focused on the man kneeling between her legs.

"Number three," he said. "This time without the ice machine. Slide up the bed and hold on for the best orgasm of your life."

Devilish green eyes stared back at her. But she was determined to show him that tonight was about so much more than her pleasure.

"Cade, how do you feel about a twofer? Number three followed by number five?"

He laughed, and the low sound left the southern half of her body clamoring for everything he'd offered.

"I'm game," he said. "But to be honest, I didn't memorize the list."

"Straight-up missionary." The simplistic drawings were imprinted in her memory. "I want to see your face, feel you move inside me while you fall apart."

A hint of wariness flashed in his eyes, and for a heartbeat, she wondered if she'd asked for too much. But she blinked and the unease had vanished, replaced by an intensity that promised she'd get her wish.

"Twofer it is," he murmured and lowered his head.

"One down." Cade trailed kisses over her hips and brushed his lips over the soft curve of her belly. His hands followed and glided up her sides.

He wanted to memorize her shape. The taste of her. The sound of his name on her lips. Hell, he wanted to bottle every sound and movement she made when she climaxed and take it with him. Her orgasms were the damn sexiest thing he'd ever heard.

"Ready for part two?" he asked as he reached her breasts, his body hovering over hers.

"Oh, God, yes," she said, her voice low and rough. "I want

more. So much more of you."

"Hold that thought. I need to get a condom."

He located another foil packet in his wallet, then covered himself and returned to her. Slowly, he sank into her, inch by inch.

She gazed down to where their bodies joined. "Your cock is perfect," she said, the bliss from her last orgasm still lingering in her dreamy brown eyes.

"Drunk on sex again?" He withdrew, just slightly. "Or are you trying to boost my ego?"

"It's your mouth." Her head fell back against the bedding. "It's intoxicating. The way you use your tongue…you have every right to feel cocky."

"I'm glad we cleared that up," he said, his voice low and raspy. He was about to come for the third time that night, but he still couldn't hold back. "I'd hate for you to leave thinking the ice machine did all the work."

Her hands cupped his jaw and held his face over hers. "No, it's you."

He stared down at her as her hips rocked up to meet him thrust for thrust. The movements felt basic, primal, and hell, when she tightened around his dick, fantastic.

But when she reached up and held his face in her hands, the rough, jagged lines on her cheek drew his attention. His jaw clenched, and this time it didn't have anything to do with the fact that he was buried inside her. He wished he could take the bastard out. Hell, he felt at home wiping out the bad guys. If given the chance, he would destroy her foster father with his bare hands. No second-guessing. No fears.

But here, making love to a woman who should be cherished, worshipped, and loved, dread rose up. Hurt and heartbreak were the last things she needed in her life. And if he wasn't careful, if he didn't make a clean break tomorrow—

"Cade! Oh, God, Cade!" She released his face, grabbed

his ass, and held tight to him.

He felt the climax overtake her body. And he followed her over the cliff, into the place where orgasms reigned without reservation.

After what felt like a lifetime of mind-blowing pleasure, he collapsed on top of her. He knew he should move, roll to one side, but his body refused to cooperate. Plain old missionary had taken everything he had.

Beneath him, she wiggled and somehow managed to escape.

"Going somewhere?" he asked, rolling to his side, wanting to see her if he couldn't feel her beneath him.

"I'll give you five minutes to recover," she said. "Before you join me in the shower."

Standing beside the bed, naked and sticky from the last round, she looked entirely comfortable in her own skin. The woman he saw now wouldn't ride him with a bathrobe tied around her waist. She wouldn't hide behind insecurities. And more than anything, he wanted her to hold on to that feeling with both hands.

"You're gorgeous," he said. "But five minutes isn't enough." After that last round, he doubted he would be able to lift his pinkie toe anytime soon, never mind the part of his body she'd just worked out.

"Are you sure?" She placed her hands on her hips. "It's time for number one."

"We need to work on your understanding of the male anatomy." He rolled to his back and stretched his arms overhead. "That's just not possible."

"Ten minutes," she said, her gaze lingering on his stomach for a second before she turned away.

He tracked her movements and followed the sway of her hips as she bent at the waist and scooped her purse off the floor. The sight of her ass in the air...

"I could be ready in eight," he conceded.

She picked a tube of lipstick out of her purse and walked over to the closet. She opened the door, revealing the full-length mirror inside. Then she used the lipstick to write their names on the mirror.

"What are you…?"

"Scoreboard," she said. Beneath his name, she added two red lipstick lines. And under hers, she added three. "Eight minutes." She placed the cap on the lipstick. "And then we even the orgasm count."

We're already even. You're forgetting about the gold-medal hand job.

"The restaurant doesn't count," she said as if reading his mind. "That wasn't on your list."

She walked out of the room without pausing, as if she didn't have a shy, insecure bone in her body—which left him with only one reason to join her in the shower. He wanted to see her kneeling on the shower floor, the water running between her breasts as she pressed them together.

He heard the water turn on and groaned.

"Time is almost up," she called.

"Temptation's a bitch," he muttered, swinging his legs over the bed. He had a feeling if he offered that explanation to Natalie tomorrow, she'd threaten to end their friendship.

The thing was that the more he learned about what had happened during Natalie's time in foster care, he realized his tough-as-nails best friend needed him in her life, too. She might scare a roomful of drunken marines, but underneath that tough exterior, he had a feeling she'd shouldered more than her fair share of the grief over what happened.

"Cade?" Lucia called. "Time's up."

He ran his hand over his face, stood, and headed for the shower. "I'm coming, gorgeous."

One more fantasy. I better make this one count.

Chapter Seventeen

Lucia knelt on the tile floor. A steady stream of water rushed over her shoulders and down her breasts. Maybe tomorrow, she'd let her body unwind again in here. But right now, anticipation threatened to twist her nerves into knots despite the warm water hitting her back. Left alone in the enormous bathroom, questions filled her mind.

Earlier, with his head between her spread legs, Cade had hesitated. Had she pushed for too much? Was she crazy to want more beyond this weekend with a man she barely knew?

He'd opened windows to his life, offered glimpses into his job and his team waiting for him back in Coronado. And he'd told her about his own parents' haunted past. He tried to pass it off like it hadn't affected him, but she saw a man grappling with loneliness. They both had their reasons for returning to an empty home at the end of the day—or deployment, in his case. But her reasons were slipping away the more time she spent with him.

When she'd planned her trip, ordering the mask and selecting her clothes, she'd hoped to find a man who found her attractive. But Cade had introduced her to other must-haves. Things like safety.

Until he'd walked into her Vegas fantasy, she hadn't realized how much she needed someone who offered both physical and emotional security. He'd given her a place to feel beautiful and wanted.

And he'd opened her eyes to the idea that desire ran deeper than perfect muscles. Sure, his abs packed a wow factor that she couldn't ignore. But the way he'd picked out a set of paints for her left her seeing so much more in him than a weekend fantasy.

The bathroom door swung wide, and Cade stepped in. She pushed her tangled mess of hair aside and focused on the very recovered SEAL standing on the other side of the glass shower door.

"Gorgeous, I want to be clear about one thing," he said, opening the door and stepping inside. "My drawings don't do you justice. Your body is a work of art."

He stopped in front of her, his feet planted hip distance apart. He trailed his index finger over her scarred cheek down to the chin. Gently, he tipped her head back.

"I will never forget the way you look right now, naked and on your knees, waiting for me," he said.

"And wet," she said, moving her hands up her body to her breasts. She cupped one in each palm and held them up, allowing the water to splash off them in every direction. "Very, very wet."

His gaze narrowed, clearly bypassing humor and heading straight for fuck-me-now lust. "Earlier, you said, 'don't hold back.'"

"And I meant it." With her breathing bordering on panting, she took in the magnitude of this moment. Cade. Here. Unrestrained. Completely hers. "But you should know, this is a first for me."

"Let me show you." His hands covered hers and drew her breasts down, pressing them together. "Hold them right there."

He wrapped his hand around the base of his cock and slid it through the wet valley. He pressed his free hand against the glass wall at his back. "Lean into me."

She tilted her body forward a fraction of an inch.

"Just like that," he gasped.

And then he began to move, his hips rocking back and forth. The tip of his cock peeked over the top of her cleavage before gliding back down.

"I don't know what it looks like from your angle, gorgeous," he said, his voice like gravel. "But from where I'm standing, this is a dream come true."

"Your number-one fantasy is everything you hoped for and more?"

His hips stilled, leaving his erection buried between her breasts. His gaze lifted to her face. "No."

She raised an eyebrow. "There's something you want more than this?"

"You." He took a hold of her hands and drew them away from her breasts. "I don't want to end the night on a fantasy."

"Oh," she gasped, confusion rushing in as he moved to the shower door.

"Don't move," he ordered. "I'll be right back."

She closed her eyes and waited. Over the shower's white noise, she heard footsteps and a tearing sound.

"Lucia." He said her name as if it were a benediction. "Lucia, look at me."

She blinked away the water and stood and moved to the glass wall and watched as he covered himself with a condom.

"I want to take you any and every way you can imagine. In public or hidden away, if it turns you on, I want to try it. And one way or the other, we'll end with you screaming my name. But right now, I don't want number one or number eleven on my list or yours."

"Then what *do* you want?"

He opened the shower door and stepped inside. "Let me make love to you. No games or Post-it note plans. Just you and me."

"Yes," she said, her voice loud and clear over the shower's spray.

He wrapped his hands around her hips and guided her back until she felt the shower wall behind her. His hands cupped her bottom and lifted her up. "Wrap your legs around me."

She obeyed, savoring the feel of his powerful arms as they so easily suspended her above the shower floor.

"This is it, gorgeous," he said, thrusting inside her, filling her completely. "This is the moment I'll take with me."

She held on tight, her thighs pressed against his hips as he began to move in and out.

I'm not going to leave you alone with memories for company. You deserve more, too.

And tomorrow, she'd tell him.

Chapter Eighteen

"You forgot to text," Natalie declared, bypassing "good morning" or "hello."

"It's eight in the morning," Lucia said. "I had a long night. And I assumed you did, too." She pinned her phone between her shoulder and ear. She used the tongs sitting beside the doughnuts to select a Boston cream, a chocolate glazed, and a powdered sugar from the buffet, then carefully moved them to her to-go container. "And I don't have much time to chat now. There's six feet plus of orgasm-inducing male perfection asleep in my bed, and I plan to tempt him with doughnuts."

"Oh my God, he trades sex for doughnuts?" Her sister's shrill voice left her wishing she could end the call right now.

"Probably." She closed the cardboard box and headed for the coffee station. "But I'm hoping he'll agree to talk in exchange for a Boston cream. I plan to discuss our future. Together."

"No, Lucia," her sister said. "You can't keep seeing him."

She set the doughnuts on the counter with more force than she'd intended as she reached for a paper cup. "You can stop worrying. And let go of this sudden interest in my life. You don't know me. Believe me. Until this weekend, I barely knew myself."

"And sex with this virtual stranger changed everything?" Natalie snapped.

"Yes, it did. With Cade, I feel beautiful and alive. And I think he feels something for me, too."

"What happens when he ships out for months on end to God knows where?"

"I wait." Lucia reached for the creamer and filled her cup to the brim. "I've endured a lot worse."

"If you want my advice," Natalie said, "you should get the next flight to Tennessee and forget you ever met him."

"Look, I know you're trying to be a good big sister. And I realize I shut you out in the past, but I know what I'm doing." She picked up the box in one hand.

"He's going to break your heart."

"You don't know that." She reached for the coffee. She and Cade would have to settle for sharing one cup. She couldn't manage two.

"Yes, I do." Natalie let out a sigh. "I need to go. But please text me when you're home. You're the only family I've got. I know I've screwed up in the past. A lot."

"It wasn't your fault." Lucia paused in the hotel hallway outside the bustling buffet and closed her eyes. It always came back to the incident. "Stop feeling guilty and just be my sister for once."

"I'm trying. I swear, I am," Natalie said softly. "I just hope you'll forgive me one day."

The line went dead. Lucia opened her eyes and moved to the windows looking out over the resort pool. She'd never blamed Natalie for what happened. Never. Why couldn't her sister accept that?

She mentally added *fix relationship with big sister* to

her list for the future, turned away from the windows, and followed the bright carpet through the casino floor toward the elevator bank. Before she fixed the past, she needed to talk to Cade about her future.

As she stepped on the elevator, she caught a glimpse of her scars in the mirrored interior.

When she'd put on the mask that first night, she'd never expected to find a man who wanted the woman hiding behind it. She'd never dreamed a man who looked like a movie star would take one look at her and label her gorgeous. But he'd proved it with every touch, every kiss, and every thoughtful gesture.

"For once, I met someone whose actions line up with his words," she murmured, stepping into the empty hall.

She balanced the coffee cup on the doughnut box and used her key card to unlock her door. She moved quietly, hoping to let him sleep a little longer. But as she gently closed the door behind her, she heard his voice come from the sitting area by the window.

"Don't you dare tell her," he said. "It won't do any good, believe me."

She remained in the entryway so as not to interrupt his call. Heck, she ought to get out of there so that she wouldn't be eavesdropping—

"It ends today, Natalie. She never needs to know you sent me."

Natalie.

No, it couldn't be. He would have told her. She'd asked him if he knew her sister and he hadn't said a word. But the pieces fit. Coronado. SEAL. Her sister's calls and texts. Natalie's concern. He *knew* her big sister.

She released her hold on the box, and the doughnuts tumbled to the carpet. The coffee followed, and the lid popped off as it hit the floor. The light and sweet liquid mingled with their breakfast.

What a mess.

"Fuck me," he said.

Never again.

His words hit her hard. Her hands formed tight fists, desperate to lash out. But then she realized Cade had stopped speaking, and when she looked up, she saw him watching her, regret and resignation right there in his eyes.

"Natalie," he murmured. "I have to go." He lowered the phone from his ear and tossed it on the sofa, then reached for his boxer briefs and jeans. Smart man. This was one conversation they couldn't have naked. "Lucia, let me explain—"

"You. Know. My. Sister." She enunciated each word to beat back the hysteria that threatened to overtake her voice. "And she sent you to find me?"

"Yes." He grabbed an undershirt off the floor and pulled it over his head. The white fabric clung to his muscular chest.

She walked through the doughnut disaster and headed for the bed, leaving a powdered-sugar trail of footprints.

The moments flashed through her mind like still images from a movie. She'd thought she was part of a love story fueled by passion. But instead, she'd been starring in a comedy/horror film. And she'd been cast in a familiar role—the girl everyone felt sorry for.

Had it all been a sham? She knew the weekend was supposed to be all about fantasies, but to think that nothing that had happened between them was real...

She sank onto the bed and buried her face in her hands. A spectator looking in might laugh at the naive woman who'd clung to the fantasy that a Navy SEAL wanted her, that he desired her. But it felt like a nightmare. The whole thing had been a lie. His reason for approaching her. For being with her. For wanting her.

"Why?" she demanded as she lifted her face from her

palms.

"Your sister was worried about you," he said. "Natalie thought you'd follow through with your plan."

"She told you I was looking to meet someone," she said, putting the pieces together. "But if she wanted someone to babysit me, why did she send you? Or was seducing me part of the plan?"

"No," he said firmly, his hands on his hips. "Natalie made me promise to keep my hands off you. But I saw you in that red dress and I wanted you."

She stared at him. She didn't know if she should be relieved her sister hadn't sent a man to have sex with her or horrified that he'd felt so damn sorry for her that he'd broken his promise.

Horrified. There was no space in this room for relief. All along she'd believed Cade was different. Being here, with him, she'd no longer felt like the girl people pitied. When the truth was, she'd been on the ultimate pity date and she hadn't even known it.

"I still don't understand why she chose you. Did she want you to string me along without touching me for the entire weekend? Did Natalie assume I'd be so grateful for your attention, I'd follow you around waiting and hoping for more?" The questions rose up one after the other.

"I'll admit your sister seems clueless when it comes to the fact that you're fucking gorgeous—"

"Cade," she protested. She wanted to erase the charade. She didn't need pet names or praise. Not now.

"You're beautiful," he said, his voice firm. "Maybe some people don't see it. But I do."

"Natalie thought I would melt at the sound of your voice, didn't she?"

He sighed. "You sister asked me to come because I was already headed to Vegas to see my dad. And because she trusts me."

"Why?" she demanded. "Are you her best tipper? A regular at the bar? Natalie doesn't let people in. Believe me. So why did she pick you?"

He looked her straight in the eyes. "Natalie's my best friend. We met when I first moved to Coronado. Two people who struggled to let others into their lives and had a commitment to remain single—we hit it off. Plus, I wanted a dog. But I'm gone a lot, so I needed someone to watch him while I was away. Natalie agreed, so we adopted from the pound."

It was as if she'd broken a dam. Now that she knew the truth, he was ready and willing to share the complete picture. How they'd grown close, their pet…

"You share a dog with my sister." Jealousy rushed in, quickly eviscerating her shock at learning why he'd suddenly walked into her life. "Wait, have you slept with her?"

"No. *No.*" His eyes widened and his fingers curled into his hips, the tension rippling through his arms. "She's like my little sister, like family."

His family.

If now was the moment for complete and utter honesty, she had to admit, if only to herself, that she'd wanted—hell, *still* wanted—more than an orgasm spree with Cade. Love, family, maybe even a pet—she'd looked to the future and hoped to find those things with him.

No wonder he'd insisted those things could never be. He'd known how much his deception would hurt her. And still he'd gone along with it.

Her hand traced the scar along her face. The knife had hurt, but his betrayal was a new kind of pain.

"You put on quite an act when my mask fell off," she said softly, her gaze dropping to the ground. "For someone who already knew what was hidden beneath. And that first night… pretending that I still turned you on after you saw my face."

"It wasn't an act. Natalie told me about your parents' car accident, and she mentioned that you'd lived in foster homes. I knew she hated the families, but I had no idea how bad it was for you. And she never said a word about your face. I swear, I never touched you out of pity."

He crossed the room and dropped down on one knee beside her. He took her hands in his and stared up at her, his expression a wide-eyed mix of desperation and determination. "I admit I've been omitting certain facts since we met, but I swear my actions were real."

She wanted to believe him, to feel the truth in his words. But he'd shattered her trust into hundreds of little pieces.

"You're my fantasy." He leaned forward, raised his fingers to the smooth skin of her unaltered cheek. And then his other hand touched her jagged scars. He cradled her face in his hands and captured her lips with his. Soft and sweet quickly gave way to something hot and needy. His tongue traced her lips, and her mouth opened, welcoming him even though her mind knew better.

The kiss deepened and drew her down with it. His hands moved down her neck, over her breasts, her sides, her hips—it was as if he wanted to map the contours of her body. As if he wanted to remember every inch of her the way she was now.

As though he knew he'd never have the opportunity again.

She lifted one arm and touched his chest. The desire was real. But as his mouth moved over hers, she realized it wasn't enough.

She broke the kiss and gently pressed her palms into his chest. Breathing hard, he released her. He stood and took a step back.

"I can't." She took a deep breath. "I want to be with someone whose words and actions tell the same story," she said, her conviction strengthening with each word.

"I know. I know."

He crossed his arms against his chest. The muscles he'd built while saving the world drew her gaze away from his face. If only bulging biceps and drool-worthy abs could be enough for her. Two days ago, they would have been. But she'd grown since then. More, she'd discovered what she wanted—what she needed—from this man. And she'd discovered how empty she felt knowing he couldn't give it.

"That's what you meant when you said I deserve more." She cocked her head, his words from last night rushing to the forefront of her memory. "I'm worthy of a man who doesn't offer lies. I shouldn't have to guess at what he's feeling." Her voice rose with each word. "Or worse, what he'll do."

"I would never hurt you," he said firmly.

"But you did," she said. Her hand went to her cheek, then touched her chest. "Just not in the way you think." Her sister had been right—this man had broken her heart. "The moment you decided to hide the truth from me, you hurt me."

"It wasn't all a lie," he said quietly. "I thought you were gorgeous from the moment I saw you staring at that painting. One look and I pictured your dress hitting the floor. And when you wrapped your perfect lips around the chocolate strawberry, I knew willpower would only carry me so far. The sex was never one-sided."

He was right. It hadn't all been a lie. The nightclub. The Bellagio fountains. Their trip to the beach. The ice machine. And the way he'd focused on her while she stroked him under the table last night. Those moments were real. She could see that.

In those moments, he'd made her feel gorgeous, pushed her to recognize the feeling and hold on to it. She would leave Vegas feeling a sense of beauty. And with a faith in herself that had been buried for too long. But that was the only thing leaving Vegas with her.

"I want more, Cade. Trust, love, a future with someone

who wants to worship me in bed and out, someone I can cherish in return. And I think we both know that I can't have that with you. Because at the end of the day, you were willing to let me leave Vegas without ever telling me the truth."

"I'm not in a position to give you what you need," he said, his jaw tight as if it pained him to say those words. "My job comes first. I knew that from the start. And I swear I never meant to hurt you."

Only lie to me.

She nodded. "I'd like to pack. I'm ready to go home now. This morning. And I need to have a few words with my sister."

"This isn't her fault," he said. "I crossed the line, turned a simple mission to keep an eye on you into something more."

"Don't you see?" she said. "I never should have been a mission in the first place."

He nodded and took a deep breath. "I know. And trust me, I plan to play that card when negotiating for visitation with my dog." His arms fell to his sides as he headed for the door. "I'll go."

The Navy SEAL, movie-star look-alike stepped over the doughnuts and headed for the door.

"Good-bye," she said as he disappeared into the hall. Call her a coward, but she didn't plan to be there when he returned. There was nothing left to say. Not when he'd proven anything more would only lead to pain.

She crossed the room, picked up her phone, and typed out a quick message to her sister.

We need to talk. But first, I have to catch a plane.

She drew a deep breath, opened the closet, and started pulling out clothes. She could walk away as if her heart wasn't breaking into pieces.

She could do this.

She had to.

Chapter Nineteen

When a mission went south, Cade shouldered his share of the responsibility. At the end of the day, it didn't matter who made the call that sent them spiraling into clusterfuck territory. He owned his share of the mistake.

He found a table in the buffet's open seating area and sank into a chair. While Natalie deserved some of the blame for sending him to derail her sister's plans, he'd chosen to fulfill Lucia's fantasy list. And hiding the truth from her? That was on him, too.

But when a mission slid into the danger zone, he started brainstorming the next step. The hostage wasn't at this location? Okay, where had he been taken? The next step was always on his mind.

Looking at this mess, recalling the stricken look on Lucia's face, he couldn't see a way out. Logic dictated that he walk away. She needed space to heal. And the strong woman who'd made it crystal clear that she should have a man in her life who offered her honest words alongside his actions—she could move on from this.

But could he?

"I haven't been to a Vegas buffet in years," his dad said, claiming the seat across from him. He set down a plate piled with eggs and bacon. He'd added one lonely piece of melon into the mix alongside a frosting-covered danish.

"Thanks for dropping everything. And for making the trip over," Cade said.

"I wasn't doing much, and you said it was important." His dad picked up his fork and knife, slicing his eggs into precise, equal-sized pieces. "Something to do with that girl?"

"She's leaving. Heading back to Tennessee," Cade said, holding back the part of the story where he'd driven her away. His dad didn't need to know the entire complicated mess right now. "And I don't want to let her go. I'm falling for her, Dad. Hard."

His father set his knife and fork aside. He raised his napkin to his mouth and nodded. "You just met her, right?"

"Yes, but the timeline doesn't change the fact that my heart is in this."

His father didn't say a word. They'd never discussed feelings. When Cade had first started dating, his dad had been away. Even after his mother left, demanding a divorce, his father had steered clear of Cade's love life, preferring to bemoan his own situation.

"Dad, I need to ask you something." Cade sat back in his chair, arms crossed over his chest. "If you could go back to before Mom left, would you do anything different?"

The room buzzed around them as people made their way back and forth to the buffet. But Cade kept his gaze fixed on his dad, waiting for his answer.

"I was willing to give my life for my country," his father said, his voice weighed down by a familiar sadness. "Looking back, I should have been willing to put a helluva lot more on the line for the love of my life."

"Why didn't you?" Cade demanded.

His dad shrugged. "At the time, I thought she could wait. I knew I'd retire eventually and then we'd be together. I turned a blind eye to her loneliness. And when she tried to tell me, I didn't listen. I saw other spouses coping, and I guess I figured she could, too."

After a moment's silence, Cade said, "Go on."

His dad stared at his plate. "Some women embrace military life. Your mother did for a while, but five years in, with a baby at home, she asked me to choose her. And I told her I would. She waited, and another twelve years down the road, she realized I meant I would choose her eventually. And she left."

Which left you bitter. You held it against her, never accepting your role in the failed marriage.

"If I had to do it all again, I would have tried to find another job. I love my country. But I realized too late that I love your mother more." His dad picked up his fork and pushed a strip of melon around his plate. "I still do, even though she's moved on."

Cade closed his eyes and pinched the bridge of his nose between his thumb and index finger. And his mind backtracked to that first night in her hotel room, after her mask had fallen off. He pictured Lucia climbing onto the bed, her breasts spilling out of the robe tied tight around her waist. She'd had every reason to distrust him, but she'd joined him on that bed, allowing him to prove his desire.

But he'd been so caught up in her transformation from a woman who looked determined to mask her flaws to the walking, talking fantasy who'd knelt on the shower floor, waiting to drive him wild with her breasts, he'd failed to see how she'd changed him.

He'd arrived in Vegas convinced long-term was off the table. His dad's misery was proof that relationships required an end date. Cade had never stopped to think he deserved more—a chance to build a life that didn't force his heart to take a backseat to his country.

He opened his eyes and stared at the old, lonely man eating a danish. Maybe his father couldn't rewrite his past, but that didn't mean Cade had to follow in his footsteps.

"I need to go." Cade pushed back from the table and withdrew his wallet. He tossed a few bills on the table.

"Going after your girl?" his father said with a smile.

"Yes. And I'm going to do whatever it takes to win a place in her life."

• • •

Lucia paced around her studio gathering paints. She pulled blues and greens, colors that stood in stark contrast to the pink hue of the sky beyond her window. Driving home from the Memphis airport, the difference between her quiet suburb and the bright lights of the Las Vegas Strip had offered a bleak reminder that the fantasy was over.

She'd stepped into the foyer of her home and dropped her bags. Without bothering to change out of the jeans and T-shirt she'd worn on the plane, she'd headed straight for her studio. The large room off the kitchen was lined with windows on one side and canvases on the other.

She selected a sixteen-by-twenty-inch canvas and set the blank surface on an easel. She needed to add one more after portrait. A complete one, portraying the man torn between what he wanted and what he couldn't have. He'd walked into her life a hero, the shining star of male perfection. But beneath his muscles, his sinfully sexy voice, and his I'll-save-the-world attitude, he was just another person struggling with the past, trying to do his best.

On the flight home, she couldn't escape the lingering

questions. How far did the lies go? She believed him when he'd said the seduction wasn't part of the plan. But what about the other little moments? What about—

Her landline phone rang. She walked to the desk by the window. She recognized the number. Natalie. She pressed the speaker button.

"I made it home safe and sound," she said, moving to the shelves lined with paint jars. "You can stop worrying."

"Lucia, I'm sorry."

A dog barked in the background, and Lucia's hand froze on a bottle labeled purple. "Is that the dog you share?"

"Yes. That's Mufasa, our Great Pyrenees," Natalie said. "Though I think he's more mine than Cade's, especially after what he did. He promised he wouldn't touch you. And he doesn't go back on his word. Ever. If he says he is going to do something, he stands by it. I thought I could trust him."

"Me too," she murmured, selecting a brush from the mason jar beside her work sink. "Me too."

"I should have come up there myself."

Her hand froze, the brush submerged in a pool of red paint. "Why didn't you? If you thought it was so important to keep me from picking up a guy, why didn't you come yourself?"

"You wouldn't have listened to me," she said.

"Because I barely know you anymore." Lucia lifted the brush to the canvas. "You never even mentioned your best friend or your dog."

"I'm trying to give you space. I wanted you to rebuild your life free from the past," her sister said. "Those families, even the well-meaning ones, they stripped away our voice in our own lives."

"We were kids," Lucia countered. "It was their job to be the parent."

"But they weren't our parents," Natalie said, enunciating

each word as if she needed someone to hear and understand her. "They didn't love us."

"I miss them, too. Mom and Dad." Lucia glanced up. The painting Cade had asked about last night, the one where each brushstroke expressed just how much she missed her parents, hung on her wall. "But I love you, Natalie. And I always will."

"Forgive me?"

"Yes," she said. "But I might not tell you where I'm going the next time I decide to take a vacation. And one day, I'll get you back. I'm not sure how, but I'll find a way."

"I've given up on men, so if you're thinking about sending a friend to California to seduce me, it won't work."

Lucia gave a mock sigh. "Then I'll have to think of something else."

"There's one more thing. And remember that you just promised to love me forever," her sister said quickly.

"Natalie—"

"Cade called and asked for your address in Tennessee."

"And you gave it to him?"

"After what happened, he owes you flowers and chocolates at the very least," Natalie insisted.

"We said our good-byes," Lucia insisted. "Cade doesn't owe me anything."

Except the one thing he can't give me—a future together built on love and trust.

"After lying to you? We both owe you a lot more than chocolate," Natalie said. "I wanted to let you know so you weren't wondering how he got your information. I know it might seem hard to believe right now, but he really is a good guy."

"I know," Lucia said. "Not everything was a lie."

"He cares about you. He wouldn't go anywhere near a spa if he didn't."

"The spa wasn't exactly the first example that came to

mind." Lucia swiped her brush over the canvas.

"Spare me the details. The idea of my sister and my best friend…I don't want to think about it." The dog began barking in the background. "I need to take Mufasa out before I head to work. Talk to you soon?"

"Yes."

After ending the call, Lucia returned to her canvas, determined to paint one last memory of her Navy SEAL before she locked him in the past. She raised her brush—

And the doorbell rang.

Cade.

No, it couldn't be. But who delivered flowers at this hour?

She held the paintbrush in one hand and headed for the front door. She turned on the light in the foyer. Staring through the peephole, she spotted the man who'd turned her life upside down over the course of a weekend. He wore the same clothes he'd had on that morning, his duffel slung over his shoulder.

Her gaze shifted to his hands. She'd never been so happy to note the absence of chocolates. He hadn't followed her across the country to beg forgiveness with sugary treats. He'd come just for her.

She opened the door with her free hand. "Just the person I wanted to paint."

Chapter Twenty

On the flight from Vegas, Cade had played this scene out over and over in his mind. It almost always began with Lucia demanding to know what he was doing on her doorstep. He'd prepared for anger, wariness, or even a door slammed in his face. But her words caught him by surprise.

"Paint?" he said.

"I started another portrait of you, and I'd love to work off the real thing." She held the door open wide. "Please, come in."

"I'll play model for you if you promise to hear me out," he said, stepping into her home. He raised his hand, wanting to reach for her and draw her close. The desire to kiss her nearly overrode logic. But first he needed to give her words, not actions.

"Deal." She closed the door, turned the lock, and walked past him into the hallway.

He followed, surveying the space. From the outside, her brown, one-story ranch appeared ordinary. But inside, the rooms overflowed with color.

"Your kitchen walls are bright red," he said.

"I like bold, vibrant wall colors." She opened a door on the far end of the space. "But I keep my studio white. A blank slate."

She led the way into a square room that had probably served as a dining room at one time. Windows lined the long wall, offering a view of the moonlit trees in her backyard. And the floor had been stripped down to the plywood subfloor.

"Stand over there." She pointed to a space in front of the easel holding a canvas.

Cade obeyed, turning to face her, his arms at his sides. "Like this."

"Hmm." She tapped the end of her brush against her lips as she slipped behind the canvas. "Perfect."

"Ready to listen, gorgeous?" The pet name rolled off his tongue, and he swore he saw her face soften.

"Yes." She dipped her brush in the paints and focused on the canvas.

"For a long time, I held tight to the belief that a relationship wasn't in the cards for me," he began. "I saw what happened to my mother each time my dad deployed. Her loneliness was like a living, breathing thing residing with us."

"And that made you believe you can't be with anyone?"

Cade inhaled. He'd planned to focus on his feelings for the woman holding the paintbrush. But the whys and hows that had pushed him to this place spilled out.

"I looked at my mom, and I wondered how my dad could ever be worthy of her love. By the time I joined the Navy, I thought I had it figured out. A person had to choose one or the other. And hell, at eighteen, I wasn't looking to settle down. I've carried that belief with me for a long time. And when I met you, I held on tight to it. I've watched countless friends' marriages implode and listened to my dad bitch about his fate for so many years."

He couldn't be sure from this angle, but he thought he heard her brushstrokes stop. Was he getting through to her?

"What about this weekend?" she said.

"I thought that I only had a couple of days to leave you feeling worthy of love without your mask. But I never stopped to think *I* could have a different future."

Her hand stopped the rhythmic dance between the paints and canvas. She peered over the edge of her work in progress and murmured, "Go on."

"I made a few calls while I was waiting for my flight," he said. "There's a Navy base not far from here in Millington. It wouldn't happen right away, but I might be able to transfer to a recruiting position at the base."

"You're a SEAL," she said. "The best of the best—"

"I think there are some marines and maybe a handful of Army Rangers that would disagree with you."

She stepped out from behind her canvas. The paintbrush dangled from her fingers. "You can't leave your team. If it wasn't for me, you would stay. You would be out there, fighting for freedom in places where children are forced to carry guns, to become soldiers."

"Or I could be here, with a woman who helps injured, abused, and sick kids find a way to express themselves." He squared his shoulders. "I don't want to look back and realize I followed the wrong path. So if you can forgive me for hiding behind my fears, for keeping my connection to your sister a secret, then I choose Tennessee. I choose you. I choose *us*. Above everything else."

She stepped behind the canvas, her brush raised, and Cade waited to see if he'd convinced her to let him back in.

Part of her wished she could abandon her painting and run

to him. But she needed to be certain the pieces lined up. She wanted to hear the words and feel his desire from head to toe.

"I forgive you," she said. "I know what it's like to let fear rule your life. And it isn't easy to let go of it."

"Thank you," he said.

"But I need more."

He clasped his hands together, as though in prayer. "Anything," he said.

"Take off your shirt," she ordered, dipping her brush in the paint. "And let me finish my portrait."

He raised an eyebrow. "Is that your way of saying you choose me, too?"

"No. It doesn't work for this portrait," she explained.

He laughed as he grabbed his plain gray T-shirt behind his head and pulled it off. He tossed the shirt to the studio floor, put his hands on his waist, and squared his shoulders. The position highlighted the muscles in his arms and chest. And those abs—she questioned her sanity, painting him instead of touching.

"Better?" he asked.

"Yes." She stared at the V-shaped muscles disappearing below his jeans. "I think this painting would work better as a nude."

"You're the artist." He kicked off his sneakers and reached for the front of his jeans. A heartbeat later, his jeans and boxer briefs landed on top of his shirt.

She stole a quick peek around the side of her easel at his semi-hard cock. "It might help if you touched yourself," she added.

He wrapped his hand around his hardening length. "Like this?"

"Yes," she murmured as her need to join him simmered. She focused on the lines and shapes, trading out her thick brush for one with a thin tip.

"Paint fast," he said, his voice rough with desire. "I don't know how much longer I can keep going like this."

"I have faith in your endurance," she said. "But I'm almost done." She ran her brush over the canvas one last time. "I can fill in the details later."

She set the paintbrush down and stepped back, briefly admiring her work. It needed shading and a few touch-ups, but those could wait.

She moved out from behind the easel and pulled at the bottom edge of her paint-splattered T-shirt. Before Vegas, she would never have stripped off her clothes under the harsh studio lights.

"Lucia?" he said, his hand moving faster up and down his erection.

"When I'm with you, I feel beautiful—"

"You are," he growled. "Whether I'm with you or not, you're gorgeous. One look and every damn fantasy I've ever had runs through my mind, all starring you. But I didn't come here for sex, or to show you how much I fucking want you."

"I know." She undid the button on her jeans, drew the zipper down, and shimmied the fabric over her hips. She kicked her pants aside and faced him in the black lace bra and panties she'd bought for Vegas. "I've replayed every moment in my head," she said, drawing her bra straps down her shoulders. "The way you allowed me to bind your hands and ride you, the ice machine, and the shower last night—I don't doubt your physical desire."

"Good."

"But I want an equal partner." She looped her fingers beneath her thong and stepped out of her underwear. "A man who won't withhold the truth."

His gaze locked with hers. "Never again."

She moved close enough to touch him but kept her arms at her sides. "Someone who wants to make decisions with me.

Can you do that?"

"Yes." He released his cock and closed the space between them, the hard planes of his body pressing against her soft curves. He wrapped one hand around her hip, the other reaching up to cup her damaged cheek.

"Where do you think we should put the painting?" she asked. "I'd like to keep this one just for us. Maybe the bedroom?"

"What color are the walls in your room?" he asked.

"Not mine. I was thinking your bedroom. In California."

"Wouldn't be my first choice." He stroked the curve of her hips. "I'd have a helluva time explaining that to my team when they drop by."

"We'll close the door," she said.

His hand stilled. "Lucia—"

"I appreciate your willingness to move your life and job to Tennessee." And she hoped it spoke to his feeling for her. "But I'm sure there are children in California who would benefit from art therapy. I'm good at what I do, Cade. I can find another job." She smiled at him. "You met me halfway. Now let me meet you."

"I love you, Lucia."

Those words.

From this man.

Her body wanted to melt into him as she screamed, *I've fallen in love with you, too!* But she wanted more than a declaration.

"I swear I will take care of you. I'll be the man you want, gorgeous." His lips brushed hers, stealing a soft kiss before pulling back. "In Tennessee or California, it doesn't matter. I want to be with you. And I promise, this time, my actions and words will line up."

She placed her hands on his hips and ran them around to his butt. *Next time, I'll paint his backside.* He was perfect, every inch of him. And he was hers.

"Let me show you," he said, the sound of his voice teasing and taunting the parts of her body begging her to drag him to the floor, declare her love, and ride him until they both came hard and fast.

He drew her arms down, away from him, and stepped out of reach.

"I don't need a bed," she said, her low tone leaving no question that she wanted him. *Now.* "You can bend me over my worktable or take me on the floor."

He cocked his head and studied the long, narrow wooden table cluttered with paints and tools. "Tempting," he murmured.

He walked over to the far wall where she'd lined up her canvases by size and shape. At the far end, she kept a couple of large pieces of fabric draped over a pole. He pulled one down and tossed it over his shoulder. On his way back to her, her grabbed two bottles of paint off the table, one purple and the other bright pink.

"Cade?"

"Patience," he said, tossing the canvas to the floor. He set the bottles down and went to work arranging the fabric like a picnic blanket. He stood up and admired his work before retrieving the purple paint.

"It's my turn to paint you." He opened the first one and poured it into his palm. He set the bottle on the ground at his feet, then dipped one finger in the paint and brushed it across her breast.

Her nipple formed a tight peak, begging for more. But—

"Those aren't body paints," she said. "They're not toxic. But they're not exactly easy to get off."

He wrapped his paint-filled palm around her breast, and then he covered her skin in a large, purple handprint. "We'll take a long bath afterward, and I'll clean every inch of you."

"We might be purple for days," she gasped as he rolled her nipple between his thumb and finger.

"Please. Let me show you how much I want you." He moved close, one hand turning her breast purple, while the other drew tantalizing circles around the nipple still reeling from his touch. "On the canvas."

She glanced at the canvas. The thought of creating art with him thrilled her. She moved to her shelves, dancing out of his reach, and retrieved two shades of blue to complement the purple and pink.

"I'm in," she said, squirting the darker blue onto her hand. "But I get to play, too."

"I was hoping you would."

She walked around to his back and ran one finger through the paint. "I love the lines of your body," she said, trailing a blue line over his shoulder blades. "The way your shoulders taper down to your waist. And God help me, your ass is a thing of beauty."

He let out a low, throaty laugh. "Right back at you."

She pressed her paint-covered palm onto his skin and left a handprint on his right cheek. She walked in front of him, scooped up the bright pink, and poured a pea-size amount onto her index finger. Then she leaned forward and traced the V-shaped muscle running down his hip.

She stepped back to admire her work. "That's one of my favorite parts of you."

"Don't ignore the others," he murmured.

She placed her palms flat on his abdomen, ran her hand up to his shoulders, and moved her body close to his until she pressed up against him. His pink and blues mixed with her purple, the colors transferring between their bodies.

"I'm crazy about your mouth." She brushed a kiss over his lips. She opened her eyes, looked up into his, and recognized the desire burning bright in him. "And the pieces of you I can't cover in pinks and blues."

"Gorgeous, you can paint my dick magenta if it turns you on," he said, wrapping his arms around and holding her close.

"Not that part," she said with a laugh. "It's the way you made me open my eyes to my own beauty. How you listen to me, never allowing the pieces of my past to cut into your desire. I fell for the man who saw me for who I am and liked what he saw."

"I *love* what I've learned about you," he said firmly. "And I can't wait to discover more."

She ran her hands up to his face, her fingertips brushing his jaw. "I love you, too."

He leaned his forehead to hers. "I was hoping you'd say those words. Wherever we go from here, promise me, we'll hold on to that love. With both hands. Whatever it takes."

"Promise." She broke away from him, picked up the blue paint bottle, and knelt on the canvas. "Now let's make a piece we can proudly hang in our living room."

He shook his head. "We'll never be able to have company again. One look at it and I'll get hard at the memory."

"Come down here," she said, patting the canvas. "And tell me all about your living room sex fantasies."

"Doggie style. Straight-up missionary. You on top." He picked up the pink. "I want it all. With you."

Epilogue

Cade stared at the Great Pyrenees in the backseat with the same cold, hard, don't-mess-with-me look he reserved for the men entering BUD/S training. But Mufasa simply opened his mouth and offered a doggie smile before shifting his focus to the cardboard box beside him.

"No, boy," he said. "That's not for you."

Hell, he should have cleared his gear out of the Jeep's trunk before he picked up the box containing a hollow chocolate strawberry. But he only had a short window—forty-eight hours—before he deployed again. And he needed to make this happen now.

"When Lucia comes out of the bar," he explained to the dog, "I'm going to get out of the car. Don't even think about touching the box. Don't put your paw on it. Don't drool on it. Got it?"

Mufasa cocked his head toward the box as if to say, *This box? The one that smells like sugar and chocolate?*

"I should have sent you to Natalie's for the night." The giant dog crossed one paw over the other and rested his head on top. And Cade softened. "Yeah, I want to spend my last few days with you, too, buddy."

Out of the corner of his eye, he saw the front door to Bottoms Up swing open. Lucia headed for the car, her long skirt billowing around her legs.

Every. Damn. Time. It didn't matter if he'd been deployed for a week on a training mission or away for a few hours. If he saw her, he wanted her. Her curves, her smile, her full, sinful lips…

He needed to pull himself together. He had a plan, and it didn't involve a quickie in the Jeep. He slid out of the driver's side—eyeing Mufasa in the backseat—and went around to open her door.

"My sister has lost her mind," Lucia said. She stopped in front of him, rose up on her tiptoes, and pressed a kiss to his lips.

"What happened?" he asked as she pulled away and settled into the passenger seat.

She waited until he'd climbed behind the wheel and held out her hands. "Natalie insisted we use her day off to get our nails done. I think she's worried I haven't forgiven her. But I have. You need to talk to her."

"I'll give her a call later." *To say thank-you.* And reaffirm his promise to live up to his end of the bargain. Natalie had demanded that he muzzle his teammate Jack the next time they visited Bottoms Up. No come-ons. No one-liners.

Three more turns and they pulled up in front of the single-story house with the fenced yard. Moving quickly, Cade hopped out of the car, gathered the box, and herded the dog to the front steps. He turned his key in the lock and froze.

"I know you hate surprises, especially when they pile up," he said, glancing at Lucia over his shoulder. "So I'm telling you now that I've added one more fantasy to my list."

She raised an eyebrow. "Do I get a stick-figure drawing?"

He chuckled. "Not this time. But before we go any farther, you should know, there's chocolate in the living room."

The woman he loved placed her manicured hands on her hips. "Open the door."

He obeyed and allowed her to lead the way, followed by Mufasa, who thank God headed straight for his dog bed and the bone Cade had left there. Lucia disappeared into the living room, but he remained by the door and freed the chocolate strawberry from the box.

"There's a fountain beneath our painting," she said, glancing over her shoulder as he walked into the room.

"Taste it," he said.

She held her finger under the flowing milk chocolate for a heartbeat and then slid it between her lips. She ran her tongue up her finger, swirled it around the tip, and traveled down the other side.

He gritted his teeth. His dick begged to join the chocolate party. But first, he had to give her the strawberry.

"You forgot the fruit." She lowered her hand. "We might have some in the fridge—"

"I didn't forget." He moved to her, close enough to touch, and held out the berry. "Take a bite."

She wrapped her mouth around the tip of the milk chocolate berry, her gaze locked with his. The structure broke as she pulled back. She raised a hand to her mouth and laughed. "It's like one of those hollow bunnies."

"Look inside."

Her brow furrowed as she dipped her fingers into the chocolate berry and withdrew a diamond ring.

"Cade?" she said, her eyes wide.

He lowered down on one knee. He set the chocolate strawberry aside and took her hand. "I have one more fantasy on my list. You in my bed, gorgeous. Tonight. Tomorrow. Forever. After each mission, I want to come home to you. And when I retire, I want to spend the rest of my life by your side."

"Oh my God," she murmured, her gaze shifting away from his to stare at the diamond ring.

"Lucia," he said. "Will you marry me?"

"You… You…" Lucia drew a deep breath, hoping to steady her trembling voice. She hadn't gone to Vegas looking for this. She'd been happy enough to find desire, acceptance, and love in one weekend, let alone the time they'd found together in the months afterward. And now, the SEAL with the panty-melting voice was offering the promise of forever.

Awe, excitement, and love formed a tangled knot in her throat. She glanced up at the painting hanging on their living room wall. The piece they'd created when he'd flown across the country determined to declare his love.

"Cade, I was yours from the moment you made love to me on the canvas." She knelt in front of him and held out the ring. "Yes, I'll marry you."

"Yes?"

She heard the echo of disbelief in his voice, as if he still couldn't accept the fact that he'd managed to merge a long-term, loving relationship with his call to serve.

"I'm going to marry you," she said firmly, offering her hand.

He slipped the ring onto her finger. Then he reached up and cupped her cheeks, drawing her mouth to his. He kissed her hard and long, as if savoring the taste. She placed her palms on his chest. She wanted more, so much more before her fiancé—

Oh, God. She knew just what to do. She opened her eyes and broke the connection, just for a moment.

"I'm adding to my list." She pulled her shirt over her head. She tossed it aside, then stood and stripped off her skirt.

"I'm listening," he said.

She unhooked her bra and drew it away from her breasts. His eyes tracked her movements, and his body tensed as if preparing to pounce and devour her. Never in a million years would she tire of the way this man looked at her—of the way he made her feel.

Desired. Cherished. Loved.

"Cade, I want to make love to you." She held up her left hand and wiggled her manicured fingers. The square-cut diamond perched on the silver band caught the late-afternoon light slipping through the drapes. "Wearing only this ring."

"Gorgeous, I'm your man."

Acknowledgments

When I sit down to write, I have a clear picture of the scene in my head. Thus, when it came time to craft my acknowledgments, I imagined writing a few witty paragraphs. I tried channeling clever but touching Oscar speeches. And I sought inspiration from my fellow Brazen author Samanthe Beck. (Have you read her clever acknowledgments? I'm tempted to send her random gifts in the hopes of receiving humorous thank-you emails. She's brilliant.) But in the end, the picture in my head looked more like an ugly-cry acceptance speech. Maybe next time I'll nail humorous. But for now, I'm sticking to straightforward and heartfelt.

First, I owe my agent, Jill Marsal, a huge thank-you for helping shape the idea for the Sin City SEALs series.

To Heather Howland, thank you for adding me to your list of amazing authors, and for working your editorial magic on this story.

To the team at Entangled, thank you for everything you do behind the scenes to produce these books and get them out to readers.

To my husband, thank you for watching the kids while I write and for tackling the mountain of dirty dishes. I hope you know how much I appreciate your support. I've tried to tell you, but I generally end up in tears with a goofy grin on my face.

And last, but certainly not least, to my readers—thank you. I couldn't do what I love without you!

About the Author

Sara Jane Stone lives in Brooklyn, New York, with her very supportive real-life hero, two lively young children, and a lazy Burmese cat. When she is not finger painting with the kids, she loves writing sexy stories, staying up past her bedtime reading red-hot romance, and chatting with her readers on Facebook.

If you love sexy romance, one-click these steamy Brazen releases...

LOVER UNDERCOVER
a *McCade Brothers* novel by Samanthe Beck

When timid yoga instructor Kylie Roberts is forced to step into her twin's sexy stilettos, she isn't prepared for the dead body in the parking lot—or ridiculously hot detective Trevor McCade. It's only a matter of time before Kylie's awkward attempts at seduction land her in Trevor's bed, but how long can a good girl from a small town hide her identity from a big city detective?

HER FORBIDDEN HERO
a *Heroes* novel by Laura Kaye

Former Army Special Forces Sgt. Marco Vieri has never thought of Alyssa Scott as more than his best friend's little sister, but her return home changes that. Now that she's back in his life, healing wounds he never thought would heal, will he succumb to the forbidden temptation she presents one touch at a time?

Down for the Count
a *Dare Me* novel by Christine Bell

After Lacey Garrity's wedding day goes horribly, adulterously wrong, she shucks her straight-laced life and accepts a reckless challenge from sexy boxer Galen Thomas, her best friend's older brother. The dare? Take him on her honeymoon instead, but will running away with the enemy lead Lacey to love?

Caught
an *Elite PR* novel by Clare James

PR professional Vivian Blake is in trouble. Her newest client, race car driver Jarod Cage, is Hot. Haaaaw-awt. And his sex tape (she has to watch them, honest) makes Viv's unused engine bits overheat big time. Now she has to find a way to salvage his sponsor and his racing career. Not so easy when the sexy chemistry between them is total carnal combustion. But when you go this hard and fast, putting on the brakes is the most dangerous thing you can do...

Seducing Cinderella
a *Fighting for Love* novel by Gina L. Maxwell

Mixed martial arts fighter Reid Andrews needs to reclaim his title. Lucie Miller needs seduction lessons to catch the eye of another man. They agree to help each other, but by the end of their respective trainings, Reid and Lucie might just discover they've already found what they desire most...